WRATH
OF THE
ANCIENTS

CATHERINE CAVENDISH

Praise for *Wrath of the Ancients*

"Like the darkest stories of Poe, Stevenson, and Doyle, it is a slow-burning tale of claustrophobia, madness, secrets, and myths."
– Beauty in Ruins

"The apprehension was so intense that I kept looking up from the book, checking every dark corner in my room, making sure no portraits were staring at me."
– Black Magic Reviews

"If you're looking for a great horror book to read, look no further! *Wrath of the Ancients* has all the ingredients for a spooky tale!
– Mello and June

"An atmospheric gothic horror tale that effortlessly blends together history and the supernatural to create an unsettling horror story that will appeal to almost any horror fan."
– The Horror Bookshelf

"In a world of zombies, vampires and prehistoric sea creatures, *Wrath of the Ancients* is a breath of fresh air."
– 2 Book Lovers' Reviews

"Catherine Cavendish delivers the disquiet and the dread - two things I love."
– Cedar Hollow Reviews

Dedication

For Colin, without whom…

Prologue

Taposiris Magna, Egypt, 1908

Emeryk Quintillus squinted up at the vivid blue Egyptian sky. Not even a wisp of a cloud marred its azure perfection, and the sun beat down, baking the desert in its relentless, searing heat. The merest hint of a breeze whipped up a small shower of sand, coating his long, dark jacket in a pale layer of dust. He brushed it off and took out his Hunter watch from his waistcoat. Midday. Not long now. He replaced his watch in his pocket. Nearby, his horse whinnied and thrashed its tail.

All around Quintillus, a small army of Egyptians dressed in traditional gallabiyahs while they carted away buckets of sand and stones, working in relays as they had done this past three months. The dig had gone well, far surpassing what their employer had anticipated. Soon, if his calculations were correct, they would find the culmination of his life's work—the tomb archeologists the world over had been searching for this past two thousand years.

Quintillus inhaled the dry air that caught in his throat and burned. He seemed oblivious to the discomfort. His surroundings were of far greater interest. The vast, ruined temple of Taposiris Magna—with its soaring stone pylons—had witnessed burials, ceremonies, battles, and destruction, but now it was about to give up its greatest secret. And, so far, the news had been good. Long-buried artifacts—small alabaster statuettes, coins, all from the right period—all depicting that enigmatic face.

Around him, the laborers sang their work songs. Different—but somehow reminiscent of—the ones he had heard black slaves sing in the cotton fields of Mississippi long ago, in another lifetime. Quintillus reached into the inner pocket of his jacket and removed a black leather-covered cigar case. He opened it and selected his habitual long, thin cheroot. A shot of blue flame from his silver lighter ignited the tobacco, and he inhaled. In his distinctive black stovepipe hat, with his long dark hair flowing over his shoulders, he presented a curiously eccentric figure in the white heat of the desert. He made no concessions either to location or temperature and appeared never to experience extreme heat or cold. But then, there was much about Dr. Quintillus that he chose to keep to himself.

A sudden whoop startled him. The Egyptians were shouting. Waving and excited. *Now.* It must be now.

The familiar rotund figure of Max Dressler scurried as fast as the heat and his out-of-condition physique would allow. Unlike his employer, he was dressed for the climate, complete with pith helmet. He came closer, panting and wiping the sweat off his face and neck with his oversize handkerchief.

Quintillus tossed the remains of his cigar onto the sand while the man recovered himself sufficiently enough to speak. The archeologist could afford to be patient for a few more minutes, after so many years of searching.

Max Dressler's breathing returned to something approaching normal and his face drained its vivid red hue. The handkerchief flapped like a white flag while he gesticulated toward the deep shaft of the dig. "We've…found…her."

Dr. Quintillus' lips twitched in the birth of a smile. "You are sure?"

"Beyond question, Herr Doktor. The sarcophagus carries her cartouche."

"And is *he* buried with her?"

Dressler's extra chins wobbled as he shook his head. "He may be in another chamber, but he is not there. Not at her side."

Quintillus's smile became a broad grin, lighting up his bearded face. "So, they were wrong. Then let us go and meet our queen."

Dressler stepped aside. His master strode past him. The narrow, steep stone steps presented no difficulties for the tall scientist, but

Dressler struggled down them. Quintillus ignored him, his mind focused on one mission.

At the bottom, the recently excavated chamber reeked of kerosene from the hurricane lamps, which illuminated it and cast deep shadows in the corners. The stillness hung heavy. It seemed to be waiting for something to break it, and the temperature was many degrees cooler down there than on the surface. Quintillus's leather boots crunched sand on top of stone. His footsteps echoed off the stone walls.

Maybe a dozen skeletons, their ruined ancient robes hanging off them, lay haphazardly on the floor—the bodies of the queen's faithful servants. Quintillus ignored them and made straight for the sarcophagus at the far end of the tomb. Propped up against the wall behind it stood an exquisite gold coffin lid, with the queen's perfect image inlaid with lapis lazuli, emeralds and rubies. Savoring this precious moment, Dr. Quintillus gazed at it, excitement mounting inside him, his blood pumping hard.

He approached the sarcophagus. The stench of the long-dead body reached him. Max Dressler, a few steps behind, smothered his nose and mouth in his sweat-drenched handkerchief, but Quintillus barely noticed the odor of decay and mortification. He leaned over the coffin and peered down at the blackened mummy.

Quintillus bent down to kiss the ancient queen on her cold, dry lips. Dressler retched.

"She is remarkable," the doctor said. He straightened. "Her state of preservation is better than any I have seen."

Dressler removed his handkerchief to speak. "But, Herr Doktor, how can you bear to…to…" He replaced his handkerchief as another retch overcame him.

Quintillus smiled. "How could I not kiss the greatest queen who ever lived? All my life I have waited for this moment."

Dressler shook his head, clearly too overcome to protest further.

Dr. Quintillus gazed back down at the queen. She had been tightly bandaged, although, by now, the material had blackened and frayed with age and the preservatives used to mummify her. Her arms were crossed over her breast. In the dim light, something glinted. The doctor reached in and gently eased her hands apart. Just enough for him to remove a small gold statuette. He recognized the image immediately. Set. Egyptian god of desert, storms, war, and chaos, who had murdered his brother Osiris and hacked his body to pieces. He turned the statuette over in his hand. The sculpted figure was of a male human from the neck down, but its head was unlike any known animal. It resembled a jackal, but one with a much longer snout. Its ears were rectangular, protruding out of the top of its head and the creature carried a staff in one hand and an ankh in the other.

The statuette felt cold to the touch, but Quintillus's palm tingled where it lay. He dropped it into his right-hand pocket.

Dressler gasped. "Did you feel that?"

"What?"

Dressler's eyes were wide. Frightened. "A breeze. No, it's gone now, but I could have sworn…"

"You have a vivid imagination, my friend." Quintillus had felt it, too. Exactly as he had expected. The god still guarded the queen. The discovery he had made all those years ago, which had led him to Taposiris Magna, yet again proved its worth. Now his new work could begin.

Quintillus returned to his queen. Her cheeks were sunken, dried out, hollow. Her eyes shut. Clumps of black hair lay around her head. Impossible to tell now whether she had been a beauty, but to the doctor, she was the most enchanting creature he had ever seen.

He checked his pocket watch. Twelve thirty. He could delay no longer.

"The men are all still here?"

"Oh yes, Herr Doktor. I have obeyed your instructions most faithfully. They have been told if any of them leave now they will not be paid."

"Good. You have done well, Dressler."

"Thank you, Herr Doktor."

Quintillus removed a small silk bag with a drawstring from his jacket pocket and held it open in his left hand while, with his right, he probed under a frayed and worn wrapping covering the mummy's breast. Feeling around he pulled out a handful of gray dust and carefully poured it into the bag. He repeated the gesture of collecting and depositing a dozen or more times until satisfied he had sufficient for his needs. Dressler watched as if he couldn't tear his eyes away. His mouth hung slightly open at the curious sight. Let him. Quintillus had no reason to explain his actions to anyone. Least of all this unimaginative little man.

Quintillus pulled the drawstring tightly shut and dropped the little bag back in his pocket.

He kissed the queen once more. "Good night, Cleopatra, my queen. I return you to your rest."

A sigh echoed off the walls.

Dressler was visibly shaking. "You must have heard that, Herr Doktor."

"Heard what, my friend?" Quintillus had to leave, but to give any indication of the urgency of their need to depart would only spook this man and he must have his willing cooperation a little while longer. Until his work here was complete.

Dressler stared at him, seemed about to say something but then shook his head. Once again, he mopped his face with the sodden handkerchief. He stepped back to let Quintillus pass.

Both men blinked rapidly in the fierce and unrelenting sunshine. The noise of the Egyptian workers had risen to a cacophony as they celebrated the greatest archeological find in a century or more. Soon they would be rich. Their fathers and mothers would be rich. Their sons and daughters would wear fine clothes.

Quintillus understood every word. His Arabic was fluent, even down to the colloquial Egyptian dialect. He smiled in their direction, lit another cheroot, and took a few, fragrant puffs.

"Order them down to the chamber," he said to Dressler who seemed to have largely recovered from his edginess in the tomb. "Tell them they can pay their last respects to their queen."

"At once, Herr Doktor."

Dressler ferried the men down the steps, ordering them in his faltering Arabic. One or two protested, but the little man shoved them forward, with surprising physical strength. Dr. Quintillus smoked his cheroot and waited until they were all down there. He beckoned

Dressler back over and the little man scurried the few yards across the sandy stone.

"Herr Doktor?"

"Seal the tomb."

"But Herr Doktor—"

"Do it."

"Yes, Herr Doktor."

Now perhaps his assistant would realize why Quintillus had ordered the massive slab to be sited in such a way that one man could set it off down the steep incline constructed next to the steps. All Dressler had to do was release the lever. He did so and the slab thundered down the descent. Too late, the workers realized what was happening. Their terrified screams reached the surface. A juddering crash cut them off. The slab had sealed the entrance of the chamber.

Max Dressler returned to Quintillus's side, panting. His face had turned puce with a mixture of fear and the effort of his labors. His eyes were wide and bloodshot.

Dr. Quintillus stubbed out his cigar butt and reached into his jacket once more. He pulled out a little silver pistol.

Dressler whimpered. "Herr Doktor?"

A shot rang out and the small man crumpled to the ground, shot through the heart. Quintillus rolled his body to the edge of the incline and kicked it. Within seconds, Max Dressler lay against the slab.

The archeologist stepped back. Under his feet, the ground trembled, then shook. He mounted his horse. The animal was spooked and Quintillus spoke soothingly to it, calming it, stroking its ears. The rumbling grew louder, and the ruined temple shook. Slabs fell from the walls. A pillar collapsed concertina-like in a cloud of dust and sand. The entrance to the chamber was now buried deep under a ton or more of stone.

Dr. Quintillus smiled. He had fulfilled his purpose here. The queen at rest again, with an army of new servants to keep her company. In his pocket, the statuette shifted.

"Don't worry, my friend, all will be as it is meant to be."

He urged his horse into a gallop and headed back to Alexandria.

Part One
1913

Chapter 1

Holland Park, London

On a chilly January day, with a stiff breeze blowing around her, Adeline Ogilvy stood in front of the shiny black door to the offices of the Sinclair Agency and smoothed down her straight navy-blue skirt. She removed the glove on her right hand and checked below her smart new hat for any stray hairs. Finding none, she examined her fingers. Nails short, of course. How any woman could type with long nails had always been a mystery to Adeline. Shame about the little red mark where she had caught her finger under one of the typewriter keys. It would soon heal, but it *would* have to happen when she was being considered for a new, longer-term position. In Vienna, too.

Adeline had always dreamed of visiting the elegant Austrian capital ever since her Viennese grandfather used to regale her with tales of his childhood there. She had been a fascinated little girl, sitting cross-legged on the rug in front of the blazing log fire in his tiny cottage. To please him, she always called her grandfather "Opa" in the Austrian way.

Opa told her about the sad old Emperor who had lost his son and heir when Crown Prince Rudolf committed suicide in 1889. Later, when she was in her teens, Opa had tears in his eyes when she went to visit him one day. When she asked him why, he said it was because he had learned that the beautiful Empress Elisabeth had been stabbed and killed by a crazed assassin. "Who will look after the poor Emperor now?" he asked, his accent more pronounced than usual.

Opa had been dead these past ten years, but Adeline had always hoped that one day she would see his beloved Vienna. If this appointment went well, she would have the chance to not only visit but live there, for three months. Maybe she would even get to see the Emperor taking his daily constitutional in the Schlosspark, accompanied by his special friend, Frau Schratt. Opa had never mentioned *her*, of course.

Adeline replaced her glove and reached up to the polished brass door knocker. She gave it two smart raps and a couple of minutes later, a smiling young woman in a maid's white cap and apron over a black dress, looked enquiringly at her.

"I am Mrs. Ogilvy. I have an appointment with Miss Sinclair."

"Very good, madam. If you would like to come inside."

The hall smelled of lavender and beeswax, and the comforting aroma continued into the office. At her arrival, the proprietor—Miss Emily Sinclair—stood up from behind her oak desk.

"Ah, Mrs. Ogilvy, how nice to see you again. You are keeping well, I trust?"

"Very well, thank you," Adeline replied.

Miss Sinclair motioned her to sit on a leather-upholstered chair opposite her and sat back down. She was a woman Adeline gauged to be maybe twenty years older than herself, making her around fifty-five. Her iron-gray hair was neatly caught up in a smart, easily managed bun and she wore pince-nez on a gold-colored chain around her neck. Whenever she needed to read anything, as she did now, she would perch the pince-nez on the end of her nose.

Miss Sinclair raised her eyes from the papers she had been studying and let the pince-nez drop around her neck. She smiled, transforming her normally pinched look. "Thank you for coming to see me so promptly, Mrs. Ogilvy. I mentioned in my letter, this is a most unusual position, and I wouldn't normally offer it to a married woman, but you are simply the only person I have who fits the stipulations of the client."

Adeline clasped her hands in her lap, feeling her wedding ring through the leather of her gloves. She took a deep breath. "I am actually a widow, Miss Sinclair. My husband was killed two years ago in a road accident." She didn't go into detail about the runaway dray horse that had trampled James to death.

Miss Sinclair switched off her smile. "Oh dear, I am most dreadfully sorry, I had no idea."

Adeline smiled. "No need to apologize. I haven't been working for you very long, and the subject has never come up."

Miss Sinclair visibly relaxed and the smile returned. Back to business. "You are aware, the position necessitates that you live in Vienna for a period of not less than three months, starting as soon as possible. I'm afraid you will find it most awfully cold there in January."

"I'm sure I shall survive. I'll make certain to take plenty of warm clothing."

Miss Sinclair smiled. "That's the ticket. You will be living in the house of the late Dr. Emeryk Quintillus. It is his commission that you will undertake, as the executors of his considerable estate have instigated this contract. By all accounts Dr. Quintillus was a most unusual man. No one even appears to know precisely where he came from originally." She perched the pince-nez on her nose and glanced back down at her notes. "He spoke a number of languages fluently including English and German, both of which he managed with no trace of an accent, although it's likely he came from neither country. Nor was he born in Austria. He also spoke Arabic, Classical Greek… Oh, and Hungarian, so maybe he came from there." She shrugged. Her clear, hazel eyes met Adeline's blue ones. "Anyway, he was an eminent historian and archeologist, specializing in Egyptology. I understand he made some significant finds over the years." She peered down at the sheets of paper in front of her. "Quite a number of years actually. More than you might think from his photograph, which was taken a few months before he died. In 1910."

Miss Sinclair handed over a sepia photograph.

Adeline took it from her and inhaled a sharp breath. "Oh my. He certainly had an individual style, didn't he?" The bearded face peered at her. The hooded eyes seemed to be guarding some secret. He was dressed in flamboyant style with a long dark coat, stretching down below his knees, a waistcoat that looked like it might be made of velvet, a white shirt with an elaborate dark cravat, and hair worn unfashionably long that extended way past his shoulders. On his head, a taller-than-usual top hat, reminiscent of the trademark stovepipe version worn by Abraham Lincoln, added to his eccentricity. The slightest of smiles played around his lips, adding to the impression of someone hiding something. There was something cruel about the set of those lips. Ruthless. This would not be a man you would willingly antagonize.

Adeline shivered and handed back the photograph.

Miss Sinclair looked at it again. Judging by the downturn of her lips, Adeline didn't think she approved of Dr. Quintillus overmuch.

"I would have said this man was no more than say, forty," Miss Sinclair said. "Yet apparently he supplied the museum in Berlin with some Egyptian artifacts back in the 1870s, so he must have been in his… Gracious, he must have been over sixty at least, maybe even older when this was taken."

Adeline shook her head. "Surely not." The man in that picture had certainly managed to preserve his youthful appearance. His face showed barely a wrinkle, but his eyes seemed to hide so many secrets — secrets Adeline didn't wish to even guess at — cruelty to match his lips, and a darkness of spirit. She suppressed another shudder.

Miss Sinclair sighed. "Ah well, the poor man is dead and buried now. I believe he had no relatives, no one knew exactly how old he was, or really anything about him, so his gravestone, wherever that is, must be pretty empty."

Although curious to know more about this extraordinary man, Adeline was even more concerned to learn about the job she would undertake. "What will I be doing for him?"

"Apparently, Dr. Quintillus wrote his memoirs not long before he died. In English, thankfully. He specified that he wanted them to be typed up by a British woman who would live in his house and be looked after by his remaining servants. He made arrangements for the successful candidate to be quite generously rewarded. I submitted your references to his executors — a legal firm in Kensington — and they responded positively and promptly. They were particularly impressed by the work you did for Professor Jakob Mayer in the Department of History at London University. They felt this, plus your other credentials, provided a near perfect match to their late client's requirements. In short, Mrs. Ogilvy, the job is yours if you would like it. They merely requested that you should make all haste to sort out your affairs here and travel to Vienna."

Adeline resisted the urge to jump up and throw her arms around Miss Sinclair. With great effort, she controlled the excitement corkscrewing up her body. "I shall be delighted to accept their kind offer," she said.

Once again she was treated to Miss Sinclair's brilliant smile. "Excellent. I can tell you that they said you were by far the best qualified candidate."

"That is most gratifying," Adeline said, still fighting hard to keep her joy under control.

"Now to the practicalities." Miss Sinclair once again planted her pince-nez on her nose and flicked over a couple of sheets of paper. "They will pay all necessary travel and lodging costs for the journey. You will proceed by ferry across the Channel and then by train to Vienna. The house is in an area called Hietzing which is, so I understand, a rather upper-class district."

Adeline smiled. The news kept getting better. "I know of Hietzing. My grandfather used to work in the Schönbrunn Palace, which is around there. He told me of his walks on his days off and all the fancy ladies and gentlemen he used to see."

"Well, it sounds as if you'll feel right at home." Miss Sinclair handed her a card, on which the address had been written in neat handwriting.

A few minutes later, Adeline Ogilvy received some puzzled looks from passersby when she half-skipped down the road, a silly grin on her face. For the first time in over two years, she felt the exhilaration of true happiness.

Chapter 2

Hietzing, Vienna

Adeline pulled the collar of her woolen coat closer around her neck in a futile effort to keep out the biting wind of a freezing January day. Opa had been right about the fearsome Vienna winters. London had been cold, but this…

Her boots crunched snow packed on ice as she made her labored way from the tram stop to the house where she would spend the next three months. The elegant mansions with their Biedermeyer architecture seemed majestic and grand after her humble terraced house in Wimbledon. The heavy, cloud-covered skies were darkening. She rested her small suitcase on the step and rang the bell of the impressive, white-painted house. A moment of panic. Should she have gone to the tradesmen's entrance, wherever that was? The Viennese were such sticklers for propriety, and their codes of social etiquette were even more stringent and proscribed than those she had been used to at home. Too late now, though. She heard the scrape of the lock. She would have to brazen it out, if necessary.

A tall, thin man, probably in his sixties, with a hooked nose and sunken cheeks, stood blocking the entrance. Judging by his immaculate black tailcoat, waistcoat, and high, starched collar, he was the butler. Butters. Unusual name. Miss Sinclair had told her he was British.

He inclined his head but otherwise remained expressionless.

Adeline cleared her throat and wished her nose wasn't bright red. She couldn't see it, but it would be in this weather. She hesitated.

Should she introduce herself in German or in English? After all, they were in Austria. *"Guten Tag, mein Name ist Frau Ogilvy—"*

"Yes, madam, we are expecting you," the butler said in clipped English. He took her suitcase from her and stepped back to let her in.

"Thank you." Adeline stepped into the warm hall, glad to be out of the cold.

"Your coat and hat, madam."

Adeline handed the garments to the butler. Still no change in his expression. Did the man ever smile?

A door to the side of the entrance opened and a diminutive maid with an earnest expression and a slightly askew white cap took the garments from the butler. She immediately hung them on the hall stand and scurried back to wherever she'd come from.

"You're Mr. Butters, I believe?" Adeline told herself to stop being so in awe of this man who was in no way her social superior either in London or in Vienna.

"Just Butters, madam. Please, come this way."

Adeline glanced around her, taking in her surroundings. The hall was an almost perfect square, with a wide sweeping staircase, black and white tiled floor and oil paintings of rural landscapes adorning the walls. In the center stood a highly polished mahogany table on which an enormous Chinese vase took pride of place.

"Ming dynasty," Butters said. "The late Dr. Quintillus liked to collect fine pieces on his explorations."

He opened a tall, dark wooden door and Adeline entered a library the size and scope of which she had never seen before. "Oh, my goodness. This is magnificent."

At last, a flicker of a smile turned up the corner of Butters' lips. The high-ceilinged room was lined with rows of leather-bound books. A spiral, wrought-iron staircase led to the upper levels and a set of library steps enabled the less accessible shelves to be reached in safety and comfort. High above, a sumptuous Egyptian scene adorned the white ceiling. A great queen seated in a golden barge.

Adeline craned her neck to take in its beauty.

"The arrival of Cleopatra at Tarsus," Butters said. "A little fanciful perhaps, but the master liked it well enough. He commissioned it to be painted by a local artist, Herr Gustav Klimt."

"I am afraid I haven't come across him. My knowledge of art is rather limited." Adeline wished she hadn't spoken so freely. The butler's expression had returned to its stony norm. Clearly, now she had arrived in Vienna, she had better start catching up with current developments in art and culture, and this Herr Klimt seemed an excellent place to start.

She followed Butters over to an antique partner desk on which she recognized the major tool of her trade. Her portable, if cumbersome, typewriter.

"I'm so glad that arrived safely. I was a little concerned."

"It was delivered with your trunk yesterday, madam. The maid has hung your clothes in your room and she will escort you there in a few minutes, in order that you might rest after your tiring journey."

"Thank you, Butters." A rest would be welcome. After two days' rail travel, sleep in a comfortable bed that didn't keep rocking would provide a welcome change.

"Dinner will be served for you in here at seven p.m. prompt. You will take breakfast in here at eight thirty every morning, and commence work at nine, except weekends when you will be free to pursue your own interests. The late master's instructions were most explicit on the subject, even down to the food you should eat. He was a most particular man. Every morning, I shall set out your work for the day and collect your finished pages at five o'clock. I trust that is all clear."

Adeline stared at him. "Perfectly." Opa had told her the Viennese liked their formal routines. It appeared this household ran in keeping with its city of residence. She supposed the free weekends were a nod at their other famous love—that of *Gemütlichkeit*, the untranslatable word that encompassed joy, pleasure, contentment, and happiness. No doubt she would get used to it. At least there could be no room for not understanding what was expected of her.

Butters inclined his head a fraction. "Very well, madam. I shall tell Magda to come to you. She is Hungarian but speaks enough English for you to understand each other."

Adeline knew her German was perfectly adequate, if a little rusty, and heavy on the English accent. "Does she speak German?"

"Of course, madam."

"Then I am sure we shall understand each other perfectly."

"Yes, madam."

Had her sarcasm been lost on him? She doubted it. Since she started this line of work after James died, she had endured a steady stream of officious butlers.

After Butters left, Adeline wandered over to the shelves behind the desk. With relief, she noticed that many of the titles were in English. She might speak and read German, but for her leisure time, it would be more relaxing to read books in her native language. The library seemed to have some order in it. She found a section on poetry and drama. Milton rubbed shoulders with Dryden. Farther along, Shakespeare nudged Marlowe. Maybe somewhere, she would find some lighter bedtime reading.

A voice startled her. She spun on her heel.

"Madam. Please, if you like to come."

"Danke, Magda. Aber wir können deutsch zusammen sprechen."

A look of relief spread over the young girl's face. Magda was clearly relieved she would be able to conduct their conversations in German rather than in a language she undoubtedly—at best—struggled with. There was the added bonus for Adeline that she could show that self-satisfied butler that his condescending habit of only speaking English to her, was entirely unnecessary. Adeline smiled to herself. Butlers!

Magda led Adeline up the staircase and then up another flight to the top. From past experience, Adeline guessed she had arrived at the floor where the servants' quarters were situated.

"How many are employed here?" she asked.

"Only Mr. Butters, the cook and me. There used to be more when Dr. Quintillus was alive, but most of the house is shut, so there isn't the work."

"Did you know the late doctor at all?"

Magda stopped in front of a white painted door, in a nondescript white painted corridor. She shook her head. "No, he died before I was taken on."

Inside, the room was surprisingly pleasant. Windows looked out over the main road to a long, yellow-painted wall that stretched as far as Adeline could see in both directions. Behind it, snow-laden trees waved in the wind, each gust sending white showers in all directions.

"Is the Schönbrunn Palace behind that wall?" Adeline asked.

"Yes, madam. And the grounds are called the Schlosspark. You can walk there on pleasant days. I often go there. I see the Emperor sometimes. From a distance, of course."

Magda joined Adeline at the window. "It's very pretty there, especially in the spring and early summer. So many flowers—and such beautiful colors—but in July and August it can be unbearably hot."

"I doubt that I shall still be here then. I am only supposed to stay for about three months and then I'll have to return to London. What about you, Magda? Where are you from?"

The girl's eyes clouded over. "A small village on the outskirts of Budapest."

"You must miss your home very much."

Magda sighed. "I do, but here in Vienna I can have a job. It was not so easy at home." Adeline sensed that any more questions and the girl would dissolve into a flood of homesick tears. Instead, she turned away from the window and surveyed her room. A comfortable-looking single bed stood next to a night table with candles and matches.

Magda struck a match and lit a candle. "I'm afraid there is no electricity up here, but you will find it downstairs."

"Thank you, Magda."

Magda opened the plain wardrobe to reveal Adeline's clothes, neatly hung.

"I hope everything is to your satisfaction, madam."

"I am sure everything is fine." Adeline checked her fob watch. "Thank you again, Magda. I think I shall have a short nap before dinner. I seem to have been traveling for days."

"Very good, madam." Magda left her alone.

———

Adeline lay down on the bed and stared up at the ceiling. The candlelight sent flickering shadows upward, making patterns like dancing fairies. She smiled. In that one instant she was transported back to her childhood and her home, lit by gaslight. There, on Friday nights, she would take a bath in front of the blazing kitchen fire. She would stare into the flames and imagine dragons and imps, then up at the ceiling where the fairies hopped and leaped, dancing in their merry way.

A tear formed at the corner of her eye. She had felt loved and protected as a child. And warm, always warm. Here, even though Magda had lit a fire in the small grate, its heat failed to penetrate to the far side of the room where she lay. Adeline shivered and pulled the quilt over her. Back home in Wimbledon, she had carried the lessons of her mother into her own little house. James always got up to a blazing fire in the winter and, at night, he slept in a warm bed.

Stop dwelling on the past. You have a new future now.

She turned on her side, pulled the quilt up to her chin and drifted off to sleep.

Two hours later, having located the bathroom, washed and changed into a warm navy dress, she felt clean and refreshed. Mixed emotions of apprehension and excitement thrilled her as she made her way down to the library.

Dinner was simple, but delicious. Evidently the cook—whose name she now knew to be Frau Lederer—knew her business. A tasty beef consommé, served with tiny strips of the lightest pancake and sprinkled with chives. The main course consisted of tender slices of beef, with sautéed potatoes, carrots, freshly grated horseradish and gravy. She recognized it from Opa's stories. *Tafelspitz.* The frugal Emperor's favorite dish.

By seven thirty she had finished her meal, and a long evening stretched before her. At least the electric light and generous quantity of lamps in the library made reading easy. After Butters had removed her dishes, she set about exploring the massive room.

The spiral staircase looked inviting, so she made her tentative way upward. It had been well constructed and gave only slightly as she made her ascent. At the top, her effort was rewarded with a collection of first editions of classic novels by the Brontë sisters, Robert Louis Stevenson, and countless authors she had never even heard of. She selected a book by E.M. Forster—*A Room with a View*. She had been meaning to read it for a few years. Now she would have the chance. She opened it and saw it had been published in 1908. A couple of years before Dr. Quintillus died. He evidently maintained his interest in books right up to the end.

She made her careful way back down the staircase and crossed to the desk, where she laid the book down and explored some more.

On the far side of the room, she pulled aside the heavy, velvet curtains at the tall windows which gave out onto the garden of the house. In the dark, it was impossible to see clearly and the sky had clouded over once more. Maybe it would snow again tonight.

Adeline pulled the curtains back across and noticed a small door in the corner of the room, which had so far been hidden from her view. She tried the handle. Locked. No key. Maybe…the desk.

She hurried over and opened each drawer. Most were empty, but then she found a small glass dish, on which lay a key.

Adeline's excitement grew when she found it fitted. Inside, a chill breeze startled her. It was pitch dark and smelled of disuse. Dank. Fusty. She stepped farther in and pushed the door wide open to let in as much light as possible. It didn't help a great deal. All she could see was a yellow wall and dark wooden floor. She took another step and shrieked.

Something had brushed her face. She scrabbled at it and dashed for the safety of the library. She looked down at her blouse and skirt and laughed. Cobwebs. Of course there would be cobwebs. The place had probably not been opened for years.

She turned back and peered around, this time staying on her side of the threshold. How big was that room, if it even *was* a room?

"Hello," she called, and her voice echoed off the walls.

Another breeze fluffed her hair. Adeline shivered and retreated. Just in time.

The door slammed shut.

"What…?"

She stared at it for a full minute before she realized the key had fallen out. She bent, picked it up and tried the handle. It wouldn't budge. Somehow it had locked itself. Or maybe jammed. The violence of the slam had triggered the lock somehow.

Adeline inserted the key in the lock. It turned easily. Through the open entrance, a deep guttural sigh swept into the library.

With a cry, she slammed the door shut and turned the key. This time it needed her intervention. So, slamming it did not automatically lock it.

She backed away, her heart thumping. If there had been a glass of brandy anywhere near, she would have drunk it. In one gulp. Only a jug of water stood on the table. Her hands trembled as she poured herself a glass. She drained it, and never took her eyes off that corner of the room.

You're tired. You imagined it. It's an old house with drafty corridors. In the daylight you'll be able to see what's behind there.

Or maybe she'd pretend it never happened. *If only I could. If only I could leave things alone…* But then James had always said she would make a great detective. "Mrs. Sherlock Holmes" he had called her on many an occasion when she'd got a fixation on solving some crime or another she had read about in the *News Chronicle*. His manner had told her he was only half-joking.

The next morning, a rare and all too brief glimpse of sunshine greeted Adeline when she drew back the drapes in her room. She gazed out over the road, busy with horses, carts, bicycles and automobiles all vying for position. The trees had lost much of their heavy white blankets, but the sky was already turning dark and seemingly full of yet more snow. A cloud swallowed up the last weak shaft of sunlight. Adeline shivered. Not only with the chill, but also with the excitement of anticipation. Her first day working on the manuscript of the mysterious Dr. Quintillus.

In the library, a simple breakfast of lightly boiled egg, toast, and aromatic coffee awaited her. She had downed her second cup when Butters arrived with a sheaf of papers in his hand. He wore the same dour expression he had worn the previous day.

"Your work, madam. I shall collect your transcripts at five p.m. prompt. Luncheon will be sandwiches and coffee. Magda will bring it to you in here at one o'clock."

"Thank you, Butters." Adeline folded her napkin and placed it on the table. Butters cleared the dishes and left her alone.

Adeline stood and moved around the desk to where her typewriter lay, ready for work. Butters had placed the sheaf of foolscap pages next to it, while on the other side lay a fresh ream of white paper.

She glanced over at the window. The clouds had broken and a shaft of sunlight streamed through the tall windows. On an impulse, she moved closer so she could see the door that had so unnerved her last night.

In the full glare of a bright winter's morning, everything looked perfectly ordinary. She glanced at the lock. No key. She turned the handle. Locked.

Adeline checked the drawer of the desk and found the little glass tray. Empty. Crossing back over to the window, she checked the floor in case the key had fallen out. She covered every available inch. Not there. No time to search anymore, though. It would have to keep until later. She must start her work or she wouldn't finish on time.

Back at her desk, she picked up the manuscript and flicked through the pages. A dozen ruled, foolscap sheets written on both sides in a neat, almost copperplate, handwriting. Not at all like her old professor's. She smiled. Jakob Mayer's spidery scrawl had proved a real challenge. The hours she had spent trying to decipher his work. He had been eccentric, too, but kind and always polite. Adeline had been sorry when she typed the words "The End" on his memoir. When her assignment finished, she was pleased that he seemed to want to stay in touch with her, at least for the purposes of exchanging greetings cards.

No chance of this happening in her current job, with Dr. Quintillus long dead and moldering in his grave in some unknown location.

Adeline shook her head and wound a fresh sheet of paper into her typewriter. She lined it up carefully, the way she had been taught. Nothing worse than finishing a page only to find the lines weren't straight.

Fingers poised, ready to type, Adeline began to read and transcribe.

I, Dr. Emeryk Quintillus, do hereby assert that every word I have written here is true, however fantastic and extreme it may appear to the learned reader. I do hereby attest to the discovery of one of the greatest Egyptian artifacts of our time, and indeed of centuries before and yet to come. For, on the 19ᵗʰ July, Nineteen hundred and eight, I did discover the tomb and treasures of the great Queen and last Pharaoh of Egypt, Cleopatra VII…

"Good gracious!" Adeline stared at the words, which seemed to dance on the page. From her work with Professor Mayer, she knew how archeologists the world over dreamed of discovering this elusive tomb, among many others, of course. But Cleopatra…

Adeline's mind raced. She struggled to accept the impact of what she had read. Cleopatra's tomb had been found by the man whose manuscript she was now working on, and no one knew. Except her. Surely not. These things simply didn't happen to ordinary, lower middle-class widows from Wimbledon.

There has to be some mistake. He got it wrong. The man was an eccentric. Maybe delusional. Mad even.

She would never know unless she typed his manuscript. Her fingers trembled and she fought to control them or she would miss a key and have to type the page again. Her work must be perfect.

Taking a deep, calming breath, she resumed her typing.

At Oxford University, quite by chance, I came across an ancient scroll, hidden away in a long forgotten dusty basement. Its author was not shown, but its contents immediately struck me as significant, for they pointed me in the direction of Taposiris Magna, where I subsequently found the remains of my beloved queen…

His beloved queen!

It also related the terrible fate that would await anyone who disturbed her. But I do not heed such curses.

*I knew instantly that I must take possession of this scroll
and follow its directions…*

Quintillus described how he had smuggled out the scroll under his jacket, hiding it in his rooms at the university and of how he raised money for his expedition, while somehow managing to avoid giving away any of the secrets which made his quest more certain of success than any of its predecessors'. Maybe such detail was interesting for fellow academics, but Adeline fought to stay awake, especially when lunchtime approached.

Magda entered promptly at one o'clock, carrying a tray almost as big as she was. Adeline flexed her fingers and stood, ready to move farther along the desk to eat her lunch.

"Thank you, Magda. When I've eaten, I think I shall take a stroll in the garden. Wake myself up a bit. I think I'm still a bit tired from my journey."

"Very good, madam. Your hat, coat, and boots are on the hallstand ready for you."

Outside, the cold air hit Adeline, making her cheeks tingle. She needed to wake up for her afternoon's work, and her short walk around the house into the snow-covered garden at the rear certainly accomplished that. She soon found herself outside the library windows. Adeline breathed in the fresh air, her breath clouding in front of her.

A sudden movement caught her eye. She glanced over her shoulder, then turned and stared. The little door had swung open. Now! Taking care not to slip, she hurried back to the front entrance and rang the bell. Magda let her in and handed her a key.

"Mr. Butters said you were to have this, madam, so you can come and go as you wish."

Adeline took the key from her. "Thank you, Magda."

Adeline removed her hat, coat, and boots, slipped her feet into her house shoes, and forced herself to walk normally into the library. But once closeted inside, she darted over to the window. Rank, stale air tainted the atmosphere.

Adeline stepped tentatively over the threshold, aware of her heart beating faster than normal. The light from the library penetrated just far enough to illuminate the top of a staircase a few feet from the entrance. Good job she hadn't ventured any farther the previous night or she would almost certainly have ended up at the foot of those stairs. She would need a lamp.

She turned back into the room and saw an oil lamp on an occasional table, next to a Chesterfield chair she had sat on while reading near the fire last night. She lit the wick from the flames, using a spill she found in a box on the mantelpiece.

She hurried back, her long skirts swishing around her ankles.

The lamp cast long shadows on the walls of the narrow, stone staircase. Adeline took her first tentative steps. She kept turning back to make sure her exit remained open. Her mouth ran dry. She strained to hear even the slightest sound. All remained still and quiet except for her echoing footsteps.

A narrow passageway stretched before her. So long, she couldn't see the end of it. She started along it, her lamp the only illumination. The hairs on the back of her neck prickled and goose bumps rose on her arms. Was someone watching her? There in the shadows?

"Mrs. Ogilvy!"

Startled, Adeline spun around to face the butler. His face shone white in the lamplight.

"Butters. You scared the life out of me!"

"May I ask what you are doing down here?" His voice was cold, as if he was restraining his anger.

"I'm...I'm sorry. I...well, this morning the door up there was locked and when I went for a lunchtime stroll, I saw it was open, so I came to investigate. I thought there might be a problem. Someone in trouble perhaps..."

She could see Butters didn't believe her. No doubt he thought her a nosy, interfering woman he could well do without.

"I suggest you return, madam. You have a lot of work to do."

Adeline resisted the temptation to tell the butler to mind his own business. He might be a god below stairs but her position meant he was nothing of the sort to her. But, for the time being at least, it wouldn't do to antagonize him. She bit back her words and settled for, "Yes, Butters. You're right. I do. I shall come back now."

Adeline allowed the butler to take the lamp from her and lead the way. Once back in the library, he closed the door and locked it, using the key that had somehow managed to reappear in the lock. Maybe he had a spare. Butters didn't say another word and left her to her afternoon's work.

Adeline carried on typing up Quintillus's rants about his colleagues. He didn't seem to have had much time for anyone in his own profession and scant regard for people in general. He dismissed leading Egyptologists of his day as charlatans. No, whatever the argument, he, Quintillus knew best. He even took issue with parts of the scroll, if they didn't fit with his conclusions.

> *The scroll speaks of Set the all-powerful god, who tore his own brother, Osiris, to shreds. It says that there is a small gold statue of him in Cleopatra's tomb—so powerful it can enact the powers to dispense more than one curse. A curse against the queen herself if she does not already possess the statue. A curse against anyone removing it from her grasp. But this goes against all perceived wisdom that I have noted in my researches and I am learning that there are parts of the scroll that are not infallible. I must tread warily with it, but I shall not be dissuaded by those fools who urge caution in such matters. I am a scientist. I must be bold and risk everything for my research. And for my queen…*

By five o'clock, Adeline began to feel glad she would never know this unpleasant and seemingly bitter man. He might be a professional genius, but he was certainly shaping up to be an amateur human being. He even belittled the archeologist who discovered the tomb of the great Pharaoh Akhenaten. In Quintillus's eyes, no pharaoh would ever match up to Cleopatra. No discovery would ever be greater than finding her resting place. Yet, for some reason Adeline didn't yet know, he had chosen to keep the incredible discovery to himself. Until now.

At no time did he ever speak of his personal life. He didn't seem to have one. He had dedicated his entire existence to his academic and archeological pursuits of one person—his "beloved queen" Cleopatra. The man had been obsessed with her.

Adeline was tidying her transcript and laying it crossways over Quintillus's original when Butters entered at five o'clock. He picked up the papers.

"Thank you, madam. Dinner will be served in here at seven."

"Thank you, Butters."

Not a word about her earlier misdemeanor.

She stretched stiff legs and flexed her fingers. The sun had already set half an hour before. Although she used it, Adeline had long been wary of electricity and cringed whenever she turned on a light, afraid of any sparks, especially after Professor Mayer had suffered a terrible fire when a stray wire had become damaged. She preferred the kerosene lamps, with their familiar flickering light and odor. She and James had always had those in their home and the smell brought back memories of their comfortable life together, when she kept house and he went to his work as a draughtsman.

All that had changed one spring morning in 1911 when James crossed a street on his way to work and a massive shire horse rounded a corner and barreled into him. Death would have been instant, the doctor reassured her. Adeline could only hope he wasn't just being kind.

Her parents had died of influenza in 1910 and left her a small amount of money. Children had never come along, and with careful housekeeping on Adeline's part, she and James had managed to accumulate some savings, which helped, but she always knew she would have to find a way of supplementing her meager income after her husband died. Few channels were open to her—a respectable young woman with no skills or experience—but then she hit on the idea of training to be a typist. She took to it straightaway, and her speed and accuracy put her at the top of her class. With a glowing recommendation from her tutor, Adeline easily found work through Miss Sinclair's agency and enjoyed the freedom of working on her own and not being chained to an office.

Dinner over, Adeline settled in the comfortable chair and opened *A Room with a View* where she had left off the previous day. She read a few pages and realized she had no idea what had just happened in the story. She set the book aside and stared into the fire, mesmerized by the flames, comforted by the crackle of the logs.

A scratching noise startled her. She listened. It seemed to be coming from behind the wall. She stood and moved closer. Whatever had caused it was moving around. She tiptoed along the wall. The scratching seemed always a few steps ahead of her. Rats maybe. Or mice.

It stopped.

She had turned, ready to return to her chair when it happened again. This time, over by the far wall, behind the door next to the window. She crossed the floor and listened, her ear against the wooden panel.

The handle rattled. Adeline jumped back. Surely no rat or mouse would do that. They would scurry along the floor.

Adeline stared. She licked dry lips. The handle rattled again.

Something heavy knocked against it. She jumped back. A long, low moan wafted into the room.

Adeline raced back to the fire and picked up the poker. She stood by the chair; her eyes riveted to the source of the noise.

Seconds ticked by and became minutes. Nothing.

Finally, still clutching the poker, she dared to cross back to the door. She leaned against it and put her ear up close. Still nothing.

It must have been the wind.

Mentally, she laughed at herself and returned to her book, but for the rest of the evening, her attention kept wandering back to that one corner of the room.

That night, she tossed and turned in her bed. Outside, the wind howled and rain lashed against the window.

In her sleep, her dreams troubled her. Armed with her lamp, she was back in that strange basement corridor, wandering its seemingly interminable, featureless length. Then she faced a wooden door. Just like the one in the library. She turned the handle and opened it. A whooshing sound, like air escaping, took her breath away. Inside was a room illuminated by tall, flickering candles. Each wall was covered in symbols Adeline knew from Professor Mayer to be hieroglyphics. All was still and quiet. Tomb-like. Someone came up behind her. Adeline turned and stared at the dead, gray face of Emeryk Quintillus.

She woke up with a start, sweat pouring off her. It took seconds for her to realize it had been a dream. It had been so real. She could even smell cigars. Did he smoke cigars? James did occasionally at Christmas. Someone had bought him a small box of long, thin, black cheroots. They had a distinctive aroma that Adeline had grown to like.

Adeline got out of bed, ignoring her slippers and the coldness of the wooden floor when she stepped off the rug on her way to the window. She pulled the drapes aside. Still dark. At least the wind had died down and the rain had stopped.

Once her breathing had calmed, she pulled her drapes closed and returned to bed. She shivered and pulled the sheet and blankets up around her chin. Still, the dream wouldn't leave her. It left her with one option.

She would have to go back down to that corridor and find what lay at the end of it.

Chapter 3

The next day was Friday. By lunchtime, her mind still reeled with the disturbing dream and Quintillus's continued scripted rants did little either to enthuse or calm her.

Charters tells me I am deluded to think I will find her there. He says she lies at the bottom of the sea, or else has no tomb at all. I tell him he is the deluded one...

The desire to explore that corridor almost overwhelmed her, along with the fear of doing so. With the weekend so close, it made sense for Adeline to hang on another twenty-four hours. Hopefully, Butters would have no reason to come checking up on her on a Saturday.

Friday evening brought no repetition of the scratching and moaning she had heard. The weather had grown much calmer. It reassured her that her theory of the wind causing the noises was probably correct.

She awoke from a dreamless sleep on Saturday morning. Sunshine and blue skies lifted her mood. At breakfast, Butters told her of the routine for the next two days.

"Frau Lederer would be grateful if you would inform her of any occasion when you will not require a meal. Otherwise she will continue as usual. Sunday is her day off, so Magda will prepare your meals on that day each week."

"Thank you, Butters. I intend to be out this morning. It is such a beautiful day, and I thought I would explore the city a little. Revisit some of my grandfather's old haunts. If you could tell Frau Lederer I will not be in for luncheon but will return during the afternoon. I shall look forward to one of her excellent dinners this evening."

"I shall inform her, madam."

"When's your day off, Butters?" Adeline hoped she sounded casual.

"Today, madam. I take every Saturday and one Sunday per month off. I shall be going out shortly and returning late this evening. If you need anything, Magda will be here."

After he'd gone, Adeline raised her eyes to heaven and mouthed, "Thank you!"

Even if Magda decided to interrupt her, Adeline felt sure she could fob her off with some excuse or other. She would give Butters plenty of time to leave for his day off and for Magda to complete her morning's dusting and polishing.

Meanwhile, Adeline would enjoy her tram ride into the city and the fulfillment of a lifelong ambition. To order a mélange coffee and a cake in the Café Central.

The streets of Vienna thronged with all manner of traffic—horse-drawn, mechanical, and two-wheeled. Trams clanged, sending pedestrians scattering off the tracks. Cars weaved in and out of the paths of fiakers, omnibuses, carts, and bicycles. The mixed smells of gasoline and manure wrinkled Adeline's nose but reminded her of London. Everywhere seemed coated in a layer of dust now that the sunshine and last night's rain had melted the snow and a stiff breeze had dried up the streets.

Adeline had dressed carefully in a tailored navy skirt and fitted jacket with matching hat, black purse, and gloves. Her black button boots were highly polished and she had taken extra care to ensure her hair was carefully swept up into a tidy bun. Opa had often stressed the importance of making a good impression at the Café Central. That way, the self-important waiters would treat her with courtesy rather than their often-accustomed disdain.

She made her way past the palaces of the Herrengasse with their elaborate facades, until she arrived at the Café Central. Inside, she stopped and stared upward at the high vaulted ceiling and tall marble columns. No expense spared on the décor here. Or on the service. A waiter appeared at her elbow within seconds. The man's face betrayed no friendliness or any kind of emotion. His eyes seemed to be taking in every aspect of her appearance. Probably sizing up the amount of gratuity she might leave him, based on the quality of her dress. Adeline swallowed. She must be assertive and confident.

"A table for one, please," she said in German. "Preferably by a window."

"Certainly, madam," he replied and indicated for her to follow.

At mid-morning, the café seethed with customers, chatting over every type of coffee known to mankind. The toasted aromas of chocolate and strong fresh coffee mingled in a warm, inviting blend, enticing Adeline. The waiter pulled a chair out for her and she sat, removing her gloves as she did so. She placed them in her lap, and her purse on a chair next to her. Outside the window, people went about their Saturday business. Some carried parcels of goods from the exclusive shops on the Kärntnerstrasse.

At the nearest table, two smartly dressed men were engrossed in their game of chess. The waiter returned and Adeline ordered her mélange and a slice of chocolate cake, just like Opa used to all those years ago. A rush of emotion threatened to overwhelm her, and she reached in her purse for her handkerchief.

"*Gnädige Frau*," the chess player said, his German tinged with an unfamiliar accent. "I believe you dropped your glove?"

He handed it to her. Adeline stared at it and at the smiling man with the black hair, neat moustache, beard, and pince-nez.

She took the glove from him. "Thank you," she mumbled, managing a smile.

"Dr. Trotsky," his companion said. "Stop stalling. It's still your turn."

"Coming, Dr. Adler." The man raised his eyes to Adeline and she suppressed a giggle. Looking over, she caught his companion's eye. He smiled and nodded to her.

Dr. Trotsky gave her a little bow and returned to his chess game. Adeline's mélange and cake arrived. She took her first sip. The frothy milk on top gave way to the strong, concentrated espresso underneath—every bit as delicious as Opa had described. Her fork slid through the dark, rich chocolate cake, so light it almost melted on her tongue.

Adeline passed a pleasant hour of people-watching, during which her neighbors, Doctors Trotsky and Adler left. Both raised their hats to her as they departed. She wondered who they were. Their demeanor, dress, and the fact they were playing chess made her think they were intellectuals. The name Trotsky sounded Russian, but then, there were so many nationalities contained within the sprawling, ungainly Austro-Hungarian Empire.

Adeline longed to explore the city further, but that would have to keep for another day. Maybe tomorrow she could visit a museum or wander in one of the parks if the weather was fine. This afternoon, she had other plans.

Back at the house, Magda took her hat and coat.

"Butters is out, I believe?" Adeline asked.

"Yes, madam. He will be back late this evening."

"And when is your time off, Magda?"

"I have Wednesday afternoons and every other Thursday off."

"I shan't be requiring anything until dinner this evening. I thought I'd read this afternoon. In the library."

"Yes, madam. You should find it nice and warm in there, and there are more logs by the fire if you need them."

"Thank you." She forced herself to contain her excitement. *Mustn't hurry. Don't arouse any awkward questions or suspicions.*

Safely alone in the library, Adeline raced across to the little table, took a spill out of the box and lit it from the fire. She adjusted the lamp, noting—with relief—the bowl, well-filled with kerosene. She was ready.

Lamp in one hand, she prayed the key would be in the lock. It was. She turned the handle and it gave. A last minute thought. She removed the key and dropped it into the side pocket of her skirt. Now she would be prepared if anything tried to lock her down there.

She made her way along the narrow corridor, passing the point where Butters had intercepted her. A sense of *déjà vu* took hold. When she came to the end and faced the plain wooden door, the odd sensation morphed into shock. She was back in her dream. Or it seemed like it. Every feature looked like every other. Dark wood. Peeling plaster on the walls. Cobwebs.

It's just a coincidence. Every corridor has to lead somewhere.

The basement corridor hung heavy with silence. Adeline reached out and turned the door handle. It creaked a little. No one had been in there for a long time. She exhaled the breath she had been holding for too long. At least there was no dream echo here. No rush of wind took her breath away.

Adeline crossed into the room beyond. An atmosphere of neglect and disuse filled the stark space. The only furniture consisted of a few scattered chairs, their stuffing protruding from worn and faded cushions.

Adeline lifted her lamp higher and something ahead of her glinted. She moved closer. A picture emerged in the lamplight. Only relatively small—probably only around thirty inches by twenty—it was exquisite. Adeline stared at the profile of a striking woman, portrayed against a gold background. Everything about the picture screamed ancient Egypt. The woman's black hair was caught at the back in an elaborate bun. Around her head, she wore the royal diadem Adeline had seen in photographs of sculptures in Professor Mayer's study. The one visible eye was outlined extravagantly in black. In the lamplight she couldn't tell the color of the iris. It could have been dark brown or black or very dark blue. The high cheekbones emphasized the subject's regal demeanor and the full lips seemed almost obscenely sensual. Adeline knew if her late mother had been alive to see this, she would have been quite shocked.

The one feature marring the exquisite beauty of the woman was her nose. It was slightly too long and a little hooked. In life this would have been an elegant, poised, and unforgettable woman. The fact that she wasn't classically beautiful would only have added to her fascination.

Adeline couldn't take her eyes off her. She moved around, attempting to gain a different perspective, but the skill of the artist had created the illusion of the eye following the viewer. Who had painted such an exquisite work of art?

Adeline drew closer. In the bottom right-hand corner, she could barely make out a signature; quite faint so as not to detract from the painting itself. Gustav Klimt—the artist who had painted the wonderful ceiling in the library. But why hide such a stunning portrait down here in this forgotten room? It had been deliberately hung on the wall in its gilded frame. Here, where nobody would come and appreciate its beauty. Or maybe, one person would. And perhaps that one person didn't want to share her beauty with anyone.

Adeline peered closely again, looking for a date, but could find none.

She had no idea how long she had been down here and the windowless room began to oppress her. At least now though she knew where the portrait was and could come and see it anytime she chose. She had to find out more about it. She thought of Butters, but he would want to know why she had been down here again when he had made it perfectly clear she shouldn't go snooping about. She could ask Magda, but the girl hadn't even worked here until after Dr. Quintillus died, so she would hardly be likely to know anything about it. As for the cook, Adeline realized with a start that she hadn't even met the talented Frau Lederer.

There remained only one person who could give her any answers about the portrait and maybe even throw a little more light on the character and personality of the enigmatic Dr. Quintillus. The painter. Gustav Klimt. All she had to do was engineer a meeting with him.

But how?

Adeline turned her back on the painting and crossed the floor to the door. It creaked as she drew it closed, and a sudden waft of air broke her train of thought. It came from inside the room. If she didn't know better, she could have sworn someone had opened another door. Adeline shone her lamp around. Nothing. Just a smell she hadn't sensed before. The sickly, sweet smell of lilies.

People had brought lilies to James's funeral and Adeline swore she would never have them in the house after that awful day. Smelling them again made her heave and cover her nose with her free hand. She shut the door and sped back down the corridor.

Someone laughed behind her. A mocking sound. Adeline stopped. Listened. Carried on a few more steps. Cold breath kissed the back of her neck. She daren't turn around.

At the top of the steps, she wrenched the door open, slammed it shut behind her and leaned against it, panting heavily. She closed her eyes and prayed she had imagined it all.

Then the scratching began again; along the wall next to her.

The sun had sunk low on the horizon, making the room gloomy and full of lengthening fingers of darkness. Only her lamp and the dying fire illuminated the library, casting dancing shadows on the walls and books.

A log crackled and Adeline let out a cry. She raced over to the light switch and threw it. She blinked in the light that dissolved the shadows and set her lamp down on its table. The scratching grew louder. Like something dragging a sharp, scraping object along the walls. A knife maybe. Or a claw.

Adeline held her breath. Her heart thundered in her ears.

The door into the hall opened. Adeline let out a cry. Magda's eyes widened.

"Madam, I am so sorry. I didn't mean to startle you."

Adeline forced a smile. "No, I'm sorry. I didn't expect anyone to come in."

"I thought I would see if you wanted any tea perhaps. It's five o'clock."

"That would be most welcome. Thank you."

Magda turned to go. Adeline stopped her. "Has there been any trouble with rats or mice in this room at all recently?"

Magda looked puzzled. "No, I don't think so. Why do you ask, madam?"

"I thought I could hear scratching in the walls. Just before you came in."

They both fell silent, listening. Nothing.

"It seems to have stopped," Adeline said.

"I could have a word with Mr. Butters about it if you like."

The thought of the butler giving her one of his disapproving glances wasn't something Adeline felt prepared to court. Certainly not yet anyway.

"No, don't say anything for now. If I hear it again, maybe I'll have a word with him myself."

"Very good, madam."

Adeline put more logs on the fire and sat on the Chesterfield as she awaited the arrival of her tea.

The only sound in the room came from the crackling of the fire. The logs sizzled and the flames grew higher and hotter again.

Without warning, one log cracked down the middle sending sparks flying onto the rug where some of them smoldered. A couple landed on Adeline's skirt and she winced. She burned her fingers pinching them out. More flew out. She jumped up and stamped on them, but there were too many to catch them all in time. The odor of singed wool accumulated as she struggled to contain the myriad of tiny eruptions.

Magda entered with her tray and joined her in seconds. Together they managed to put them all out.

The rug didn't fare so well. It was covered in minute black singe marks.

"Oh heavens, Butters won't be pleased," Adeline said, hoping she sounded less disturbed than she felt.

"It isn't your fault, madam. It must have been the wood. I'll explain what happened to Mr. Butters. I'm sure the rug can be cleaned and repaired."

"In the meantime, do you have a fireguard of some sort? I'd hate for this to happen again."

"I'm sure there is, madam. I'll find it and bring it right away."

She hurried off and Adeline poured her tea. Her hands trembled and the cup clanked against the saucer. It wasn't Butters' reaction she feared, whatever Magda might think. But the way that log had cracked. The way the sparks had flown out of the fire. Something about it didn't add up. The angle of the log didn't match the spray of the sparks.

The ones that had landed on her skirt couldn't have. Not in the order of things. If someone had thrown those to one side, at an unnatural angle… Yes, that would have done it.

And what about the crack in the log itself? As if someone had taken an ax to it in the fire; however impossible that might be. The flames were burning normally now, but just before the accident had happened, Adeline could have sworn they had changed color from their normal yellows and reds to a fleeting deep purple and green.

She could keep telling herself she'd imagined it, but Adeline couldn't shift the belief she had seen it with her own eyes.

She was also sure of something else. In those flames, she had glimpsed a small, shiny, beetle and, for one second at least, it had lived in that fire. It had moved.

Chapter 4

O ver the next week, Adeline fell into a routine. It gave her some comfort to know that breakfast would always be at eight thirty. She would commence work at nine, stop at lunchtime, work through the afternoon and, after dinner, read in the quiet library. And it *had* been quiet. Since the strange noises at the weekend, there had been no scratches, and now the fireguard stood solidly between her and any spluttering logs. No more sparks singeing either her or the rugs. The damaged one had been replaced and Butters hadn't said a word about the matter.

Time and again, Adeline tried to find the right time, or the words, to ask Butters more about the mysterious Dr. Quintillus. The pages she transcribed day after day had plummeted into the realms of the all too familiar. The dry-as-Egyptian-sand narrative of the academic. Calculations, deductions, quotations from learned sources, all the sort of thing Professor Mayer had crammed page after page with and which had filled Adeline's days the previous year. Some days she fought hard to concentrate, her mind wandering off into thoughts of its own while her fingers faithfully typed sentence after sentence, paragraph after paragraph, page after page.

She carefully lined up each new sheet, wound it into the little machine and clunked away at the heavy keys. One day she calculated that if she continued at her current rate for the anticipated three months, the resulting manuscript would be something like 2,500 pages long. What had started out a promising, unique discovery had slumped into another tedious archeological expedition. Who on earth would be bothered to read such a tome?

By Friday, Adeline needed her weekend break. She had also decided she would spend it getting some answers to her questions about the portrait and the mysterious Dr. Quintillus.

At nine o'clock, Butters entered with her work for the day. The impassive face seemed incapable of movement. He placed the sheets next to her typewriter, without a word.

"Thank you, Butters," Adeline said. He inclined his head an inch and made to leave, but he wouldn't get away so easily this time. "I wonder," she said, "May I ask you something?"

He straightened his shoulders, no doubt bracing himself for some tedious enquiry.

"Madam?"

"It's… I've been typing Dr. Quintillus's manuscript for over a week and I don't feel I know any more about him than I did before I took on this assignment."

Butters' expression remained stony. "I wasn't aware that such knowledge was a requirement of your position."

Adeline chose to ignore the dripping sarcasm and pressed on. "Maybe not, but I am interested in the man who would create such a beautiful room, with such an amazing ceiling which, as you told me, he specially commissioned. Reading the newspapers this week, I know a little more about Herr Klimt and his reputation."

Butters' lip curled.

"Oh no, I didn't mean *that*." Adeline laughed. She had read some gossip about Klimt's alleged fondness for his female subjects. "No, I meant his reputation as a great, modern, reforming artist. It showed foresight on Dr. Quintillus's part to commission work from him. And such a work, too. It must have cost a fortune. The gold alone…"

Adeline allowed her gaze to travel upward, and she craned her neck to see Cleopatra with her handmaidens, gods and goddesses. For the first time, it occurred to Adeline that the model for this Cleopatra couldn't possibly be the same as the one who had sat for the mesmerizing small golden portrait she had seen down in the basement room.

She lowered her gaze and looked straight into the butler's eyes. "Were you here when Herr Klimt painted that ceiling?"

Butters nodded. "Yes, madam."

"Did he use live models?"

Butters shook his head. "I believe all that had been done in his studio. He brought pages of preliminary sketches with him and worked from those."

"And did Dr. Quintillus supervise the work at all?"

"The doctor was away in Egypt at the time. The disruption to his work would have been far too great had he remained here."

"I can understand that." Adeline took a deep breath. "Do you know where Herr Klimt has his studio?"

Butters' eyes opened wide. Surely, he couldn't have looked more shocked if Adeline had propositioned him!

"Madam, I can assure you that if you intend to visit Herr Klimt on your own, that would be most unwise."

Adeline thought quickly. She decided to take a gamble. With any luck, Butters wasn't interested or inquisitive enough to read the manuscript before he delivered it to Adeline each day.

"It's a little awkward," she said, her mind fabricating as she spoke. "You see, Dr. Quintillus included a note on one of the pages this week. Evidently, he lent Herr Klimt a small picture to work from and he requested that whoever transcribed his manuscript should ask him to return it so that it might be added to his work. He refers to it and, without it, that section of the manuscript won't make sense."

Did Butters believe her? He hesitated. Then he appeared to decide.

"If you tell me what it is, I could call on Herr Klimt myself and retrieve it."

Adeline hadn't anticipated such an apparently generous gesture. Now what would she do?

"Oh no, Butters. I couldn't ask you to do that. You have quite enough to occupy you, with this great house and so few staff. No, I can promise you, I shall call on Herr Klimt in broad daylight, remain outside, and refuse to cross his threshold. That way, no possible harm could come either to my person or my reputation. I shall probably not even see him. He will no doubt be working and his servant will attend to me. Besides, I know precisely what Dr. Quintillus gave to him. He describes it in some detail, but a little at a time. I have built up the picture of what it is, but you would have to wade through pages and pages of—I'm sorry to say this—dry, academic text." Adeline pasted on a smile. Butters wavered. It was clear he never read the manuscript and the thought of doing so…

"Very well, madam. Herr Klimt's studio is at his home on Feldmühlgasse. Number eleven. It's about a mile from here. I can draw you a map, but it's relatively easy to find, or you could take a tram. The Number 58 will take you close to it."

Relief swept through Adeline. The little lie had been worth it.

That evening, Adeline settled down with a new book. She had just begun *The Island of Dr. Moreau* by H.G. Wells—a modern author whose work she had never read, thinking its other-worldly content wouldn't be to her taste. Dr. Quintillus clearly enjoyed the author's books and this would be the first of at least twelve she could choose from. As the fantastic story began to unfold, Adeline could see why.

She had become thoroughly gripped when the scratching began again. She jumped, listened. It came again. She crept over to the window. The noise began again. This time the scratching came from the other side of the wall. Behind the bookshelves.

The small key was still in the door where she had left it.

A minute later, the lit table lamp in her hand, Adeline took a deep breath and opened the door.

The scratching stopped. She paused at the top of the staircase and rubbed her clammy palms, one after the other, on her skirt. Her mouth had dried. Nausea built up inside her. She must go on. Adeline crept downstairs. The lamplight cast flickering shadows on the wall. She caught her breath more than once at the fluttering patterns they created.

At the foot of the stairs, she paused again, listening for any noise. Nothing. Half her mind told her to go back, but the winning half pressed her onward, along the fusty corridor. No smell of lilies today.

The door stood slightly ajar. She couldn't remember if she'd left it like that.

A full three quarters of her brain told her to retreat, but the stronger, determined quarter won. Adeline pushed open the door with one finger. This time it creaked so loudly Butters must surely hear. Perhaps the butler's pantry lay above here. Or on the other side of the wall. Maybe *that* was where the scratching came from. Adeline shook herself and crept into the small room.

She shone her lamp around the walls until it alighted on the portrait.

A sudden movement grabbed her attention. On the periphery of her vision, a shadow materialized on the wall a few feet away from the portrait.

A shapeless mass at first, it began to take form. A shape that couldn't be there, because she was alone in this silent room.

Her mouth gaped at the distinctive profile of a stovepipe hat and a head with long hair. It lost its shadowiness, became clear and well-defined. A sigh echoed around the walls. She felt it on the back of her neck. Adeline let out a cry, grabbed her long skirt with her free hand and raced out of the room. The door slammed hard behind her.

Then, she was back in the library, with no recollection of getting there and nothing in her hand. She spun around. The lamp stood on the table again. Unlit. She sped over to it and reached out to touch the glass bowl. Cold. She looked around. Her book lay face down on the chair, just as she remembered leaving it before she went to investigate the noise. She looked at her watch. Ten twenty. But that didn't help. She hadn't checked the time before she went down.

Adeline returned to the door by the window. The key was still there. She turned the handle. Locked.

She went back to the chair and retrieved her book. She must be over-tired. Perhaps she had fallen asleep while reading. Maybe she had sleepwalked, although that would be a new experience. Either way, she needed to go to bed. Tomorrow, in the daylight, everything would seem much clearer.

Adeline tossed and turned. Every time she closed her eyes, she saw that shadow on the wall. The shadow that couldn't be there. She *must* have imagined it, but it was all too real. Eventually, she fell asleep, only to wake with a start.

She sat up and listened. Nothing. The servants slept on the other side of the house, so it was always quiet along her corridor and in her room. She lay back down again, only to leap out of bed. A knocking sound. Someone had banged on the ceiling of the room below. But all those rooms were shut up. Butters had told her so. Magda had told her the same thing. Dr. Quintillus would have had his bedroom down there, and there would have been guest rooms—although whether such a man ever had guests seemed unlikely.

No light crept under the drapes. Adeline struck a match and lit her bedside candle. She peered at her watch, which lay on the night-table. Five minutes after three.

She placed the candle back down. Its flickering flame caught on something on the wall. Something that glinted. Something that made Adeline catch her breath.

It couldn't be…

She picked up the candle and held it closer to the wall above the mantelpiece.

She stared.

The golden portrait of Cleopatra stared back at her.

"*No!*"

Adeline scrambled into bed. The candle fizzed out. Terrified, she buried herself beneath covers and squeezed her eyes tightly shut.

Any second, someone—or something—would surely come and get her.

But the room stayed silent. No more noise from downstairs. Eventually, through sheer exhaustion, she fell asleep.

———

For a few seconds after she awoke in the morning, she had forgotten what had happened. Then it all washed back over her and she forced herself to look over at the wall.

It was bare.

Adeline drew back the drapes and peered more closely at the space above the mantelpiece. Lacking a picture rail, the wall seemed equally bare of any nail or hook that the portrait could have hung on. The pale sunlight illuminated her room. It seemed unreal somehow. She must have dreamed it. The picture, all that banging… The shadow on the wall in the basement.

None of it could have happened. So, why was she so sure it had?

Her cheeks tingled and she felt her nose reddening in the chill air. Thankfully, the tram arrived within a few minutes and she sat back on the wooden bench seat, next to the window. A couple of stops later, she climbed down the tram's steps onto the sidewalk. The conductor rang the bell and the Number 58 clattered off. Butters' clear directions meant she quickly found Feldmühlgasse.

Number Eleven consisted of a single-story villa at the end of a narrow, overgrown path. To the left, a rose bed had been planted, with bushes that would surely be a picture in summer. The rest of the garden was lawned, with trees and flower borders. A scattering of wooden chairs and benches hinted at lazy warm afternoons, when Klimt and his guests would sip wine and talk of art. With winter still firmly gripping the city, the trees stretched out stark, skeletal fingers. The seats invited no one but the hardiest soul.

Adeline raised her hand to knock and a brief moment of trepidation almost made her turn and run back.

A meow sounded at her feet. Something rubbed against her ankle. She looked down at a small black and white cat, nuzzling her. Adeline bent down to stroke the friendly animal and the door opened. The cat trotted in, tail held high.

Adeline straightened and came face to face with a balding, well-built man, with a beard, sparkling blue eyes, and a friendly smile. He wore a bright blue smock and, despite the chill, only sandals on his bare feet.

"I saw you from my studio window," he said. "How may I help you, *gnädige Frau*?" His gaze traveled up and down her body.

Adeline had the unnerving sensation of standing naked in front of him. She cleared her throat. "Herr Klimt?"

He nodded.

"My name is Mrs. Adeline Ogilvy. I am sorry to arrive unannounced, but I wondered if you could help me with some questions I have regarding a painting you did for the late Dr. Quintillus."

At the mention of the archeologist's name, Klimt's smile froze on his face. He pulled the door open wider. "I think you had better come in."

Klimt led Adeline into a small, strikingly furnished reception room, one wall of which was adorned with brightly colored Japanese woodcuts. The furniture had been made of black stained wood, ultra-modern to Adeline's eyes, although the style was familiar. It reminded her of a photograph she had seen in a magazine, showing designs by Charles Rennie Mackintosh. Along one wall, a large display cabinet was filled to the brim with books of all shapes and sizes, demonstrating that their owner had eclectic taste in his reading material. Surfaces were covered in all manner of exotic art. Tribal masks from Africa and Asia, primitive, carved wooden statues. In one corner of the room, a complete suit of Samurai armor looked like it might march forward at any moment.

In the center, on a modern blue patterned rug, stood a small square table with two chairs. The artist motioned her to sit there and Adeline lowered herself into the chair. It wasn't the most comfortable experience, but she ignored the lack of upholstery. Opposite her, his eyes seeming to gaze into her soul, sat the only man she knew who could answer at least some of her questions.

"May I offer you some refreshment?" he asked.

"No. Thank you for the kind offer, but I must be keeping you from your work, so I had better tell you why I came so that I don't disturb you any more than is necessary."

She heard herself gabbling and willed herself to stop. She noted the artist's fingers, ingrained with a palette of colors. A strong smell of oil paint and linseed wafted in from the next room. His studio, no doubt.

Gustav Klimt smiled. "You are not disturbing me. Not at all. See? You are not disturbing my little friend, either."

The black and white cat, which had befriended Adeline on her arrival, rubbed itself against her chair leg. Adeline bent down to stroke it.

"He likes you." Klimt smiled.

Adeline smiled back. "I like cats," she said.

"Now, tell me how I may help."

Adeline wished he wouldn't gaze at her so intently. He must be in his fifties—old enough to be her father—but every time he looked at her, he seemed to undress her with his eyes. She remembered Butters' warning. She shouldn't even be in his house. She must ask her questions, get her answers, and leave.

"It's about a painting you were commissioned to do for the late Dr. Quintillus," she said.

"Which one? I was commissioned to paint two works for the doctor."

"The library ceiling is exquisite, but it's the smaller one. The golden portrait of…well, I believe it is of Cleopatra."

Again the smile creased the corners of Klimt's eyes, lighting up his face. She had clearly said the right thing.

"Thank you. I must have done a reasonable job then."

"It's the most amazing picture I have ever seen in my life. There is something…" She searched for the right word in German, couldn't find it and settled for a description. "The subject seems to be from another world."

"It felt like that as I was painting her. This was the most unusual commission I have ever had. Also the best paid. It seemed money was no object for the good doctor. He simply must have this portrait." Klimt punctuated every word with a light tap on the table.

"Can you tell me more? How and when he approached you?

Gustav Klimt leaned back, took a breath and leaned forward again.

"I completed the ceiling for him in, I think, 1905. I worked to a fairly exact brief. More restrictive than I would usually prefer, but…he intrigued me, this archeologist with an obsession for one woman. Cleopatra. He insisted on choosing the model. I objected, but I had some bills to pay and he threatened to cancel the project if I refused. When the time came to paint, I was relieved to find he would be away.

By then, I feared he would be up there, next to me, guiding my every brush stroke."

Adeline doubted the man opposite her would ever have allowed that to happen, however many bills he owed.

"He paid me, seemed pleased with the results, and we both carried on with our lives. Then, in late summer of 1908, I received a visit from his butler. Dr. Quintillus had returned from an expedition to Egypt and urgently sought my help. He wanted to commission a small portrait of Cleopatra and he was prepared to pay whatever I asked, as long as I would accept certain…conditions. I was unsure at first, but the request intrigued me, so I agreed to meet with him at his house and so began the oddest commission of my life.

"He told me he had made a major discovery. One which, if news of it ever got out, would mean he would be hounded by every historian, newspaper, and charlatan from all over the world. He didn't want that. It would interfere with his work and, besides, he wanted to keep the details of his discovery secret until after his death. He said he had made plans for that, and I should imagine you are part of that plan."

Adeline nodded. "I rather think I am. I have been commissioned to type his manuscript, giving details of his discovery. He believed he had discovered the tomb of Cleopatra."

"Yes. That became clear as soon as I began work although, naturally, he swore me to secrecy. I had the distinct impression he could be very dangerous if crossed, so I respected his wishes. He didn't threaten me, you understand. There was something about his demeanor. The intense gaze…" Klimt stared off into the distance for a moment, then shook himself. "No matter. As with the ceiling, his brief was exact. This time it was even more prescriptive. He would supply the model. More than that, he would bring her to me each morning, wait in this room while I worked and then take her home each afternoon. Maybe he didn't trust me with her." Klimt smiled. "She was a different woman to the one I had used for the library. Striking. Much as I imagined the real Cleopatra to have been. In all the days she posed for me, she never spoke. Not one word. She didn't even say anything to Dr. Quintillus. It was a strange and unique experience for me. To have no communication, no contact with my model is not my usual way of working."

He smiled at her and Adeline fidgeted. He was a charming companion, but she really shouldn't be alone with him.

He cleared his throat and continued. "When I showed the preliminary sketches to the doctor, he seemed happy and approved them. Then he did something I found so odd, I still have no explanation for it. He handed me a small silk bag and told me I should mix the contents with every color I used to paint the portrait. I must be careful to use every last bit, but to be sure and distribute it evenly. He impressed on me the importance of his instructions and checked I had understood. I opened the bag and it was half full of an ash-like powder. It smelled unpleasant—as if something had died in that bag. I wanted to refuse. After all, I had no idea what it was or how it might affect the texture or shade of the paint. He seemed to read my mind, because he set about reassuring me that it would have no effect whatsoever on the finished result. A statement that turned out to be true, fortunately."

"So, you carried out his instructions?"

Klimt nodded. "To the letter."

"Did anything...odd happen while you were painting the portrait?"

For the first time, Klimt seemed uncomfortable. He shifted in his seat. "Such as?"

"I don't really know, but it is a remarkable picture. Her gaze seems to pursue you around the room."

He seemed reassured and smiled. "A little trick. Many artists do it."

"No, I mean, this is different. The painting seems alive somehow."

Klimt ran his hands through his hair and sighed. "I'm not at all sure I can answer your question, but I will say this. I painted the portrait and was glad when it came time to hand it over and I could be rid of it from my studio."

"Why? Did something happen?"

"I am an artist. I have an artist's imagination and the circumstances surrounding this portrait were nothing if not unusual. I think my mind played tricks on me but, sometimes, in the night, I would hear noises coming from my studio. Like someone thumping the floor, or stamping. Sometimes, late at night, I would hear scratching in the walls. On a few occasions I went into my studio to prepare for my day's work, only to find the picture had moved from where I was sure I had left it."

Adeline blinked rapidly. "It's still happening."

"What is?"

"All of it. I heard someone thumping on the ceiling below my room, I frequently hear scratching in the walls, and recently, I woke up to find the picture in my room. I thought I had dreamed it, but it never felt like a dream. Now you have confirmed it."

"My dear Mrs. Ogilvy, I can't be sure I didn't imagine I had left the portrait in a different place. The scratching I heard could have been mice."

"But it all stopped when you handed the picture over to Dr. Quintillus?"

Klimt exhaled. "Yes."

"And you have never known other pictures to apparently move from where you left them?"

"No. In my experience, they tend to remain where I expect them to be." He smiled.

A part of Adeline wished those blue eyes weren't so intense. That they didn't maintain such a steady gaze at her. Another part of her welcomed it. Her cheeks flushed with a heat she hadn't felt since James died. No, she must remember why she was there. She fought off the urge to squirm and coughed. "Herr Klimt, did you ever see Dr. Quintillus hang the portrait?"

"No, I never returned to his house."

"And he never told you where he intended to hang it?"

Klimt shook his head. The cat jumped on his lap and began a deep, throaty purr. The artist tickled the furry chin.

Adeline spoke. "Would you be surprised to learn that it hangs in a dark empty basement room? That is, when it isn't appearing on my wall."

Klimt shrugged. "Little about human nature surprises me. He did pay me a great deal of money, so I would have thought he would have wanted to display it more prominently, but it is his money and his choice."

Adeline decided she had exhausted Klimt's information on that score, but there remained one more avenue she hadn't fully explored.

"The model he brought to you. Did you ever learn her name?"

Klimt shook his head. "No. I think the painting is a faithful reproduction of her looks. At least in profile. She wasn't beautiful, you understand. But she had an aura about her. I found her irresistible — except, of course, I had to contain my natural urges. I don't think Dr. Quintillus would have approved if I hadn't. I'm also fairly sure I would have been rebuffed by her, too."

Adeline squirmed again and hoped it wasn't obvious. Her cheeks flushed hot and she could see Klimt watching her reaction closely. What was it about this man? He wasn't exactly good-looking but…his eyes. Sensual. Warm. They seemed to undress her. She was stepping on dangerous ground. She gave a slight cough.

"Is there anything else you noticed about her that struck you as peculiar or unusual?"

"She wore her Egyptian robes as if she was accustomed to them. Not as a model wearing a costume and assuming a role. Her bracelets looked like pure gold and appeared authentic, and her face had a look of antiquity about it. Every age has its facial characteristics and hers didn't belong in the twentieth century, or even the nineteenth. If Quintillus had told me he had brought me the real Cleopatra, I would have been tempted to believe him."

Adeline's breath caught in her throat. "Are you being serious?"

"Most definitely. The woman who posed for me no more belonged in Vienna in 1908 than I would have belonged in Alexandria in 30 BC. And I would go one step further." He paused as if unsure whether to proceed, then leaned forward. "I would have said that Dr. Quintillus feared her for some reason that maybe even he didn't understand."

Whatever Adeline had been expecting, she could never have imagined such a response. "So, who was that woman? Where can I find her?" She hadn't realized she had voiced her thoughts, until Klimt replied.

"I doubt you will find her. Maybe I'm being fanciful, but I don't believe you or I will ever see her again. Not here. Not in Vienna."

Adeline nodded. She had to agree. But she had to know more about this strange model. Clearly, Herr Klimt had told her all he knew, and he was giving her *that* look again. Time for her to go, unless she wanted to find herself in all sorts of tangled trouble. She stood. Herr Klimt pushed his chair back and the cat jumped off, with a protesting squawk.

Adeline held out a gloved hand. "Thank you for being so helpful, Herr Klimt. It has been an honor to meet you."

He took her hand and held it between his. She felt his warmth flowing into her blood from his gentle touch. "It has been a pleasure to assist such a charming lady. May I say also that your German is impeccable. Such a pretty accent, too." Without warning, he touched the side of her face. She felt her cheeks burn.

"Now, yours is a face that most assuredly belongs in the twentieth century. It would be my pleasure to paint you."

Oh, the temptation to say, "Yes." But deep breath… "Thank you for your flattering offer, Herr Klimt, but I'm afraid my work doesn't allow me the time to accept. I do however value the honor you do me by making such a request. I hope you are not offended."

Klimt lowered his hand. "Not at all, my dear Mrs. Ogilvy. I quite understand. If you change your mind, you know where you can find me. You are always welcome here."

Once safely out of sight, Adeline stopped and fanned her still-burning cheeks. Even the chill air did nothing to cool her. On the tram, her mind filled with jumbled thoughts. The noises—and the way the portrait had apparently moved in the studio. Just as it had in Dr. Quintillus's house. Klimt's belief that the doctor feared the woman he brought to sit for the portrait was odd to say the least. Then another thought struck her. What did Dr. Quintillus die of, and where was he buried? At least she should be able to find out the answer to those two questions easily enough. Butters.

The butler's lips turned down at the corners. "Why do you ask, madam?"

"I'm curious, I suppose. Is he buried in Hietzing cemetery?"

"No, madam, he is not."

"Then where—"

"Madam, with all due respect, I am not at liberty to discuss my late employer's resting place with you. For reasons of his own, he wished its location kept secret. I do not even know its whereabouts."

Adeline hadn't expected that. "But surely you must have been involved in making the arrangements?"

Butters shook his head. "No. When Dr. Quintillus died, he left instructions with his lawyers that the house would be shut up for a month. The staff was to be given paid holiday and, on our return, we found that everything had been taken care of. Only the cook and I were to be kept on, although we were allowed to retain the services of a maid. That is when we engaged Magda."

"So, who was this legal firm?"

Butters drew himself up to his full height. "I am sorry, madam, but I am not at all comfortable discussing these matters with you. The firm was based in Kensington, in London, but I am not at liberty to divulge anything else unless you can show me that it is essential to your work which is, as I recall, typing up the late doctor's manuscript."

Impasse. Adeline stared at the butler, and he returned the steady gaze. Such an infuriating man! Clearly she would get nothing more from him. Except…

"Very well, Butters, but would you at least tell me what the doctor died of?"

"I have no idea, madam. It was sudden, and to us at least, unexpected. More than that I do not know. I suggest you occupy yourself with the doctor's work, rather than the circumstances of his death."

The butler left the library, and the temperature seemed to rise a few degrees. Probably her imagination. He did have a cold and frosty manner after all. But more importantly, had he told her the truth? It seemed incredible that even his own staff didn't know what their employer had died from, but then, so much about Dr. Quintillus didn't conform to normal standards of behavior.

After dinner, Adeline sat by the fire, reading. A few minutes later, her eyes grew heavy and the book fell on the floor.

A noise woke her and she sat up, rubbing her eyes, but stopped in mid-action. It came again. A creaking sound from across the room.

She stood and took a few steps toward the window. She stopped. Watched, in mounting horror, as the door to the basement slowly swung open.

Chapter 5

Adeline stared at the door, too scared to move. It stayed open for a few seconds and then slowly started to close. She stayed frozen to the spot. Waiting. She had no idea what for. She listened hard. What if something had come into the room? Supposing she was no longer alone in here? Beads of sweat broke out on her forehead and she licked dry lips.

Your imagination is running away with you. Someone is playing tricks. Keep calm.

If only she could convince her heart to stop thumping quite so painfully.

Then it started. The scratching. But not the same as last time. She clapped her hand over her mouth to stifle the scream that threatened to erupt.

This time, the scratching came from *inside* the room. Her terrified gaze tracked the noise around the book-lined wall behind the desk, into the far corner. It stopped. Returned. Became a distinct scraping—like a comb on a blackboard. It set her teeth on edge and she clamped her jaws together. She mustn't show fear. Do that and they would win. She would do the opposite. Take charge. "Stop that *now*!"

The scratching stopped. A woman's laugh rang out. Harsh, grating, growing louder. Adeline clapped her hands over her ears, but nothing would drown out that inhuman cacophony. Any longer and her eardrums would burst. She raced out of the library and up to her room, locking the door behind her.

Someone had deliberately set out to scare her. One of the servants? Surely they must have heard the terrible racket. Bur for the life of her, Adeline hadn't a clue who or why anyone would do such a thing. But she was determined. They wouldn't defeat her.

Adeline woke next morning, still fully-dressed and sprawled out across her bed. She drew back the drapes and a watery rising sun filtered in. It was still early. She checked her watch. Seven thirty. Time to wash and change out of yesterday's clothes. Time to think what she was going to do after the events of last night.

On her way down for breakfast, she paused on the landing of the floor below. One of those rooms had belonged to Dr. Quintillus and the more she thought about it, the more certain Adeline became that she would have to find that room and search it for any clues to unlock the mystery of whatever was happening.

The thought terrified her, but the alternative—of doing nothing—frightened her even more. That raucous laughter in the library. She hadn't imagined it. Someone was toying with her and she didn't like it. Adeline promised herself she would get to the bottom of this. Whatever the truth might be. After all, James always said she was stubborn.

Now, whoever—whatever— you are, you will see how stubborn I can be.

It was the butler's Sunday off, so Magda served her breakfast of toast, a boiled egg, and a pot of aromatic coffee.

"Is Butters out today?" Adeline asked, trying to sound casual.

"Yes, madam. He won't be back until late."

"Thank you. I shall be staying in. The weather isn't so pleasant."

"I believe it's going to rain later, so you're probably wise. It may even turn to snow again. It's certainly cold enough."

Magda left her to her thoughts and, as she finished her meal, Adeline's pulse quickened.

She pushed back her chair and, forcing her fear back down into her stomach, left the library, and mounted the stairs.

On the first floor, she pictured the location of her room above. The staircase was in the middle of the house, so there were corridors left and right of it. Both looked identical, with their dark green walls and mahogany doors, all shut tight.

Adeline turned down the left-hand corridor and started along it. She tried the first handle. Locked. Then the second. Also locked. If her calculations were correct, the third door she came to should lead to a room directly below her own. The one from where the knocking sounds had come.

She turned the handle. It opened. Taking a deep breath, she pushed it wider and stepped inside.

Heavy, polished mahogany furniture dominated the room. A red, blue, and gold Chinese silk carpet partially covered the parquet floor, and the double bed was a four poster, elaborately carved and covered with a plain deep brown eiderdown.

Surely, this masculine room must be the one Dr. Quintillus had used.

On the dresser, a glass-domed gold French-style clock ticked. The rhythmical noise soothed her a little. Adeline shivered. The neatly laid fire only needed a match to get it started, but she resisted the temptation. Even though Butters wasn't around to discover her, she would still prefer to do her explorations and get out without leaving any trace of her presence.

She started opening drawers but became increasingly disappointed. One after the other came up empty.

Even the night-table revealed nothing more than a neatly folded, fine quality gentleman's handkerchief. Adeline unfolded it and found embroidered initials, *EQ*, intertwined. Confirmation, surely, that she had the right room.

She opened the wardrobe. Also empty. Stumped, she let her gaze travel around the room, alighting on an anomaly. In the wall, next to the bed, there seemed to be a slight gap that didn't correspond exactly enough to a seam in the dark green wallpaper. It was a fraction too deeply defined.

Adeline moved around the bed until she could make out the gap. A cleverly concealed entrance. She felt down it, then across, and her fingers soon found the opposite edge. With no handle and no sign of a keyhole, how would she open it? She felt down the crack and heard a click. The panel gave beneath her fingers and she pulled it open. A puff of cold, stale air made her nose wrinkle. It smelled like mouse droppings.

She peered hard, and the light from the room was sufficient to make out the top of a staircase. It had to be an alternative route to the basement. Adeline went over to the mantelpiece and took down the kerosene lamp she had spotted earlier. A box of matches had been placed next to it and she used one to light the wick before carefully replacing the glass shade.

She made her way down the stone steps, identical to those in the library entrance. This time she had two floors to descend and when she reached the bottom, a much shorter corridor awaited her.

Adeline took care not to let her shoes clatter on the stone floor. She wanted to be able to hear the slightest noise. At the moment, nothing. She hoped it would stay that way.

At the end of the short corridor, her lamp shone on a door identical to the one she had reached through the library. It too was shut. She turned the handle and it opened smoothly. A noxious smell hit her—a stench of lilies and something long dead. Rotten. The urge to turn back almost defeated her but she had come this far, she had to find out what lay on the other side.

At first glance, the room looked much like the one which housed the picture. But, when Adeline moved the lamp around, she saw a figure seated at the table. She let out a cry and almost dropped the lamp.

He had his back toward her. Dressed in a long, dark purple, velvet jacket, his dark hair fanned his shoulders and on his head was the trademark stovepipe hat that gave away his identity. Dr. Emeryk Quintillus sat like a statue, apparently unaware of her presence.

Adeline moved closer, swallowing her fear. "Dr. Quintillus?" Her voice wavered. She tried again, moving around the table to face him, scared of what she might see, but knowing she had to.

"Dr. Quintillus, my name is Adeline Ogilvy and I...oh my God." The lamplight lit up the doctor's face. Now she could see why he hadn't reacted when she entered the room.

His beard remained attached to a face that was gray, dry, mummified. His eyes were empty, black hollows as if someone had scooped out the contents. His mouth was closed and his parched hands lay, curled on the table in front of him, the skin cracked and flaky, like plaster that had been heated too much. If those hands moved, a shower of dust would coat every surface they touched.

If they were to move… Adeline stared at the corpse. A sigh echoed around the walls.

Then the scratching began. Her lamp flickered. A woman's voice whispered in her ear. Words she didn't understand, in a language she had never heard before. Adeline clamped her hands to her ears, too terrified even to run.

The door slammed shut, opened, slammed shut again. Still, Adeline couldn't move. Her legs wouldn't obey her. She had become rooted to the spot. In the flickering light of the lamp, shadows danced on the walls. A bizarre creature with an animal head, long snout, and unnaturally rectangular ears stood on human legs and held a staff in one hand. It must be behind her but she couldn't turn to look. Its shadow shimmered and faded.

The woman's voice grew stronger, louder. She had a commanding tone, but Adeline couldn't understand one word. The door opened and slammed shut again. Once. Twice. Time and again. Adeline felt light-headed. Dizzy. On the verge of fainting.

Don't give into it. Fight. Fight!

More visions swam in front of her eyes. Real, but as if glimpsed through opaque glass. Desert sands whipped into a storm that swirled around her, then vanished. An ancient queen in a golden chariot, drawn by two black horses. Cleopatra. Her eye caught Adeline's, then looked away as if what she saw displeased her. Adeline shielded her eyes against the intense light and heat of the sun as the scene changed again. A jackal's head, its eyes flaming red, reared up in front of her, its distinctive ears and human body emerging as if out of the shadows.

Adeline became aware of another movement. At the table. Slowly, deliberately, Quintillus uncurled the fingers of his right hand. Adeline stared as his yellowed, horny nails scraped along the table's surface, gouging out deep scratches.

The creature raised its staff, as if to strike her.

Adeline closed her eyes. She heard her own voice, strong and commanding. *"No!"*

Everything stopped.

Adeline opened her eyes.

She was back in Quintillus's room, staring at the wall. The entrance was closed. Barely distinguishable. In her hand, she held the lamp, still alight.

Adeline extinguished the flame, set the lamp down on the dresser and dashed out into the corridor. Up in her room, she turned the key in the lock.

Could she have imagined what happened? But she knew it was all too real. Quintillus was in this house, in his own basement, impossibly mummified., or somehow still alive. And he wasn't alone.

The next morning, after a sleepless night, Adeline stood and waited for Butters to bring her breakfast tray to the library. He came in at eight thirty prompt, wearing his usual dour expression. He laid the tray down on the desk. Adeline ignored it.

"Butters, I made a very disturbing discovery yesterday, in this house, and I need you to accompany me."

His eyes shot open. "May I ask why, madam?"

"I'll show you. Then you'll know why. Please come with me."

Butters stomped behind her, up to the first floor, where he snapped at her. "You have no business snooping around on this floor."

"I think you'll change your mind when you see what I found." She stopped outside Quintillus's room.

Butters' face turned red. His hands shook with rage. "Madam, I must protest. You are not allowed to enter here."

"Too late, Butters."

She marched over to the far wall. The butler stood in the entrance, his hands behind his back. Adeline didn't need to see them to guess that he was clenching his fists. He could probably have willingly thrown her out of the house and might still do so for her transgression in daring to violate his late master's inner sanctum, but she didn't care.

"Did you know about this?" she asked. She found the catch and the door swung open.

"Of course. I know every inch of this house."

"So, you are familiar with the basement rooms then?" Adeline went over to the dresser, lit the lamp and picked it up.

Butters nodded. "Naturally."

"When were you last down there?"

Butters hesitated. "I really couldn't say. I have little reason to go to the rooms under this part of the house since Dr. Quintillus died."

"But you have been down there in the past three years?"

"Probably. I can't remember, and it really is no business of yours."

"Come with me." Adeline led the way.

The basement door was closed. Adeline turned the handle and it opened. This time, no smell of death and decay greeted them. Adeline took a deep breath, dreading the sight she knew awaited them.

"Perhaps you have an explanation for this?" She gave Butters a gentle push into the room.

"For what, madam?"

Adeline stared in disbelief at the table and chair. No sign of Quintillus. No gouges on the table's wooden surface. She shone the lamp around the otherwise empty room. Tangled emotions of anger and disbelief swam through her mind.

She lifted the lamp so that it lit up Butters' face. She wanted to see his expression when she accused him. "You moved him, didn't you?"

The immediate look of incredulity proclaimed the butler to either be innocent or an exceptionally fine actor. "Moved who, madam?"

"Dr. Quintillus. Yesterday he was seated at that table. He looked as if he had been mummified, his eyes had been removed and he had clearly been dead a long time. Except…" No, she wouldn't tell Butters about that moving hand. The butler was already staring at her as if she had lost her wits. "Now he's gone. Where did you take him?"

"I don't know what you are talking about, and I really must protest at this unfounded and quite disgraceful accusation."

He sounded genuinely shocked and offended. A doubt crept into Adeline's mind. What if he was telling the truth? She knew what she had seen, but if Butters hadn't moved the body, who had? Could Quintillus really be alive? And as for everything else…

"Do you swear that you have not moved Dr. Quintillus's body and that he is definitely not alive and living in this house?"

"Of course I swear! The whole idea is preposterous. The doctor was buried three years ago."

"Yet you refuse to tell me where. Why is that, Butters? I don't believe it's simply because your employer wanted to keep it secret once news of his discovery got out."

"I don't know where he is buried. We were never told."

"And you didn't think that was odd?"

Butters shook his head. "Dr. Quintillus was a most unusual man. No one knew much about his personal life, where he came from, who his family were. Deciding to keep the location of his burial secret was all part of his nature. It seemed perfectly normal to those of us who knew him or had worked for him. Now, if you've quite finished concocting outlandish theories and throwing false accusations around, I have work to do. As indeed do you."

"Where does my work come from, Butters? Where do you pick up the manuscript every day and where do you take my completed typescript?"

"That is none of your concern."

"Oh, but it is my concern. It became my concern the first time I started hearing strange noises, seeing things that couldn't be there. It became my concern when I found Dr. Quintillus's body down here yesterday."

"Not that again! You couldn't possibly have found his body down here. Where is it? He could hardly have stood up and walked away."

Adeline was sorely tempted to throw doubt on that but resisted. "Kindly answer my question."

Butters hesitated. Maybe trying to decide whether he was at liberty to reveal the answer.

"If you must know, the papers are sent to me, with clear instructions, by Dr. Quintillus's legal firm in London."

"And you are instructed how many sheets should be given to me each day?"

"Yes."

"And what do you do with my completed work?"

"At the end of each week, I package it up and send it to London. To the legal firm."

"How bizarre. You would think I could have stayed at home and typed it up there."

"Possibly. But then you wouldn't be in this house, would you? And Dr. Quintillus wanted you to be in this house."

Butters looked as if he wished he could take his last words back.

"Why is it so important that I be here?"

Butters shrugged. "I have no idea. I only know my late employer wanted it that way."

"Did he tell you that?"

"No."

"Then who did?"

"It was in the first set of instructions I received from the lawyers. Dr. Quintillus had made his wishes explicit and clear. He had charged the legal firm with ensuring everything was done precisely as he wanted." Butters folded his arms. "That's quite enough. I'm not answering any more questions. I repeat, I have work to do, and so do you."

Reluctantly, Adeline led the way.

Today's pages were more interesting than the last few days' had been. Dr. Quintillus had chosen to reveal little snippets of information about his feelings for this project.

> *I am sure we are getting much closer to my queen. I can almost feel her life-force beckoning to me, although I know that is impossible. She has been dead for nearly two thousand years, but her spirit is still so strong, so vital. When I behold her I shall be transported...*

The narrative returned to the more formal, dry, academic account of earlier pages but a few sheets later, he again chose to share an interesting reflection.

Cleopatra is always associated with the goddess Isis, but little if anything is known of her affinity to Set, the god of darkness and death. I believe I shall find the small gold statue close to her. He was to be her protector in the next world. Contrary to the threats expressed in the scroll, I believe anyone possessing this statue would be imbued with its power. The power to thwart death itself. With this statue, I will gain this strength. I must have it, as much as I must have her…

A chill froze Adeline's blood as she typed those words. Dr. Quintillus had been dabbling in dark arts. Maybe that's why she heard those voices, that scratching. If he had found the statue, it certainly hadn't helped him cheat death. She'd seen the evidence of that with her own eyes. But those words, *I must have it, as much as I must have her…* played again and again in her head. What if he had cheated death, not for him—but for her? Gustav Klimt had said that if Quintillus had told him he had brought the real Cleopatra to sit for him, he would have been inclined to believe him. But what if he had?

Fantastic and incredible it might be. But it was hardly any more incredible than what she had already experienced.

Adeline typed like an automaton for the rest of the day, her mind full of swirling, impossible ideas. By five o'clock she had decided. She needed advice from someone who knew far more about Egyptology than she did. Professor Jakob Mayer. She would write to him that evening. Maybe within a week or so, she might have a few more answers. In the meantime, she must remain calm. Outwardly at least.

––––––––

She mailed her letter to Professor Mayer the next morning and her working days once more fell into a routine. She had grown wary of the library after dark so, once she had eaten dinner, she made her way upstairs and spent her evenings reading in her room—thankfully undisturbed by any banging noises or the reappearance of *that* picture.

The weekend arrived and Adeline stayed out for most of the day. She took her meals out. No doubt Frau Lederer would welcome the rest.

Adeline explored the city her grandfather had loved so much. She strolled in the Schlosspark and even caught a glimpse of the elderly Emperor with his distinctive white beard and bushy whiskers, dressed in his military uniform and escorted by a middle-aged lady, clothed from head to foot in navy. Frau Schratt, no doubt, accompanying her friend on his daily walk.

Adeline visited the Art History Museum and marveled at the wealth of exhibits, including murals and paintings by her newfound acquaintance, Gustav Klimt.

She took coffee and cake at the Café Central, but this time Dr. Trotsky and his friend were absent. She contented herself with sipping the delicious mélange and watching the world go by outside.

Butters was barely civil to her. He seemed unwilling to engage in any kind of dialogue. Adeline responded with a polite "Thank you," but avoided making any requests of him. By contrast, the manuscript continued to grow more interesting with each passing day.

Today, the workers have uncovered a shaft, precisely at the point where I knew it to be from the scroll. The sun was already setting when they made this discovery, so we shall begin again at first light tomorrow. I felt her move through my spirit. Soon I shall behold her…

That scroll. It had to be somewhere in this house. If not in his room, then maybe in the basement. After all, she had barely searched down there. Maybe there were more rooms waiting to be discovered. But after what she had seen, she couldn't bring herself to go down there alone again. The mere thought of it sent her body shuddering and her teeth chattering. No, she would wait and see what Professor Mayer advised before she investigated any farther.

The ensuing days' manuscripts concerned aspects of the dig; precise measurements, detailed descriptions of artifacts discovered as the army of workers labored away, shifting heavy buckets full of stone and carefully sifted sand. Coins depicting the legendary queen, a small alabaster statue. All were faithfully recorded in Dr. Quintillus's neat hand.

Every day, Adeline hoped to see the small silver salver in Butters' hand that would indicate a letter from home—a reply from Professor Mayer, or so she hoped.

Two weeks went by and, finally, Butters handed her the salver. She recognized Professor Mayer's spidery scrawl immediately but was surprised to read the postmark. "*Wien.*" Once the butler had left the room, she tore open the envelope and unfolded the single sheet of notepaper.

> *My dear Adeline,*
>
> *I am most intrigued by your letter—so intrigued in fact that I dropped all my commitments and headed post haste for Vienna, where I am staying at the Hotel König von Ungarn, near the cathedral. I shall be pleased if you would join me for coffee there on Saturday of this week at 10:30 in the morning. If this is not convenient, please telephone the hotel on….*

Saturday. Just two days away. Nothing would stop her from keeping that appointment.

An almost palpable sense of relief refreshed her and washed away the perpetual lump of fear that had settled in the pit of her stomach. On more than one occasion, over the past couple of weeks, she had considered quitting this assignment and returning to London, but the thought of how she would explain her reasons to Miss Sinclair and the belief she would find herself without any more work if she reneged on such a lucrative contract, stopped her. She couldn't afford to throw this job up. Somehow she had to see it through. Until that point, she hadn't realized how scared she had become. Now, at last, she would have an ally to help her solve the mystery that surrounded Dr. Quintillus. Professor Mayer would get to the heart of it.

She sat at her typewriter and began on the day's assigned pages.

Today we will open the tomb. I have seen her cartouche. I have also seen the symbol of Set. Soon I shall see my beloved's face. But no one else will ever see her after today. No one may be permitted to gawp and stare at the greatest of them all. None but I will remember the first sight of that wondrous sarcophagus. Then she will be mine for all time. Mine alone. For he shall not come between us…

Adeline made some hurried pencil notes in a small notebook she had been compiling since she wrote to the professor. Butters would never allow her to remove any of the manuscript, and she would never remember all the important extracts to relay to Professor Mayer. At least this way she would be able to give a fairly detailed account of Quintillus's discovery and his emotions.

On Saturday, in a chilly wind and drizzle, Adeline got off the tram and walked the short distance to the professor's hotel—a smart, comfortable old building on Schulerstrasse, a narrow street a few yards from the cathedral square.

Professor Mayer was seated on a high-backed chair in the lobby. He saw her and beamed. "Dear Adeline. It has been too long." Only a faint accent betrayed his childhood in Bavaria.

He struggled to his feet. Adeline hurried to help him. His rheumatism must be playing up again. Hardly surprising in all the damp weather.

How reassuring to hear his voice. A wave of relief surged through her. Surely now he was here, everything would be all right.

"I am so pleased you came, Professor." Adeline shook the hand that wasn't leaning on his ebony walking stick.

"My dear, how could I not? You described such a tantalizing puzzle, I simply had to come along and see for myself. Besides…" His blue eyes twinkled under heavy white brows. "I could never resist helping a lady in distress, and you seemed so distressed. Come, let us sit and we'll order coffee." The waiter appeared from nowhere. Adeline ordered her now favorite mélange and the professor settled on an espresso.

Professor Mayer smoothed his neatly trimmed white beard. "So, Adeline. You are working on the manuscript charting the Egyptian adventures of Dr. Emeryk Quintillus."

"Yes. You seem to have heard of him."

"Oh indeed. Mainly by reputation. A queer bird by all accounts. At Oxford he kept himself very much confined to his rooms and his research. Made himself quite unpopular by refusing to share his findings with anyone. Reading between the lines, I think the university encouraged him to leave." The professor tapped the side of his nose and winked at Adeline.

"I'm not altogether surprised. The whole tone of his manuscript is of someone obsessed. He writes of Cleopatra as if she was some long-lost love."

"That doesn't altogether surprise me. I had guessed as much from my own enquiries. But you told me in your letter that some extraordinary things had been happening."

The waiter arrived with a tray containing two small glasses of water, some delicious-looking macaroons, and their coffee. As he laid them out, Adeline took the opportunity to retrieve her notebook from her purse. She handed it over to the professor and sipped her coffee while he read through her notes. His eyebrows rose, and his complexion grew paler with every page.

Finally he finished and handed the pad back to Adeline.

"Well, my dear, this is certainly a complex and peculiar situation to have found yourself in."

"Can you help me, Professor? I am terrified of going back down to that basement on my own, but I feel that so much has happened, I must find out the answers or this will haunt me for the rest of my life."

"Oh, indeed, you must have the answers. There is no question of that. Because, you see, Adeline, you are right. Whatever Quintillus unleashed when he found—and I believe, plundered—that tomb has attached itself to you. You were meant to find that body, you were meant to hear and respond to the noises, and you were meant to see that picture on your wall."

Adeline blinked. Her mind raced, thoughts tripping over themselves while she tried to make sense of what the professor had just said. "I am out of my depth here, Professor. This is so far from anything I've experienced before. I've always been rational. Things like this belong in stories. Edgar Allan Poe. Mary Shelley…" She shook her head. "It's been quiet these past couple of weeks. I've stayed out of the library at night and nothing has happened. Surely if anything was there it must have gone now?"

"I wish I could reassure you, Adeline, but I'm afraid all I can say is that the relative peace and quiet you are currently experiencing could go on for a few weeks more. But it will all inevitably begin again. Nothing is resolved and, if I am correct, you won't be leaving that house until it is."

Adeline stared at the professor. His face was deadly serious. Her pulse quickened. "But why, Professor? I am only there to type his manuscript. It could have been anyone."

Professor Mayer shook his head. "Oh no, my dear, it couldn't possibly have been anyone but you. You were specially chosen for this assignment."

"Yes, but only because I speak German, surely."

"The manuscript is in English. The butler is English. I am satisfied that even if you hadn't spoken German you would have been chosen for this position."

"I don't understand. Why?"

"That, my dear Adeline, is the question we need to answer."

Chapter 6

"Professor Mayer to see you, madam." Magda showed him into the library.

The professor limped in, leaning heavily on his stick. His knee obviously pained him. Adeline rose from the chair by the fire and shook his hand.

"Please come and sit down, Professor. You must be freezing. It's so cold out today. Come and warm yourself by the fire." She turned to the maid, who was leaving. "Magda!" The girl reappeared. "As Butters is away this afternoon, I really don't think he need know about my visitor."

Magda hesitated for a moment, then the briefest smile twitched the corners of her lips. "No, madam. May I get you some coffee?"

"That will be fine. Thank you."

Professor Mayer was glancing around the room. He stared up at the ceiling. "Fine painting."

"Yes, Gustav Klimt was commissioned to paint the ceiling as well as the portrait I told you about."

"Unusual style. Very modern. I'm not sure I like it, but it certainly shows talent. He is clearly very good with faces."

"Yes." Adeline smiled.

"Now," the professor said, "when we have had our coffee, I suggest we begin by visiting the basement room you can access from here. We will explore it in as much detail as we can, and then we will proceed up to the doctor's room and see what we can find both there and in the basement room that can be reached from there."

"Yes, Professor." However confident and matter-of-fact the professor sounded, it didn't stop a coil of fear beginning to twist itself around Adeline's spine.

The coffee arrived. They chatted about old times for a few minutes and then the professor gripped the chair and stood. Adeline helped him. "Thank you, my dear. These damned legs of mine don't work the way they used to. A physician friend of mine from Oxford days, suggested that one day modern materials and medical science will combine to invent an artificial joint to replace the human knee. Artificial knees! I ask you. Whatever next? Artificial hips? Brain transplants?" He laughed and Adeline joined in. Crazy talk indeed.

Adeline had pocketed the key to the basement before the professor arrived. Now she used it. She gagged at the fusty air, tainted with the sickly smell of decay and lilies. She grabbed a handkerchief from her skirt pocket and clamped it to her nose and mouth.

"Not very pleasant, is it?" The professor wrinkled his nose. Adeline picked up the lamp she had placed near the door and lit it.

"You lead," the professor said. "I'm afraid I can't be a lot of help to you at this stage. I need to hold the stair rail with one hand and my stick with the other until we get to the bottom."

Adeline tucked her handkerchief back in her pocket and tried to ignore the stench as she held onto the rail and descended the steps. They proceeded along the corridor until they reached the closed door. She turned the handle and tried to concentrate on breathing normally.

Her lamp lit up the hieroglyphic-festooned walls. But…

"I swear they weren't there before. The wall was bare—except for the portrait."

"Gracious!" the professor said. "Come closer with your lamp, Adeline. I need to make out these symbols."

He peered closely. Adeline brought the lamp as near as possible. "'To speak the name of the Pharaoh is to make her live again. I speak the name of'… This is indistinct…but I believe he meant to give the cartouche of Cleopatra."

A loud sigh echoed around the walls.

Adeline nearly dropped the lamp. "Did you hear that?"

The professor nodded and carried on reading. "'Homage to thee, Set, oh god of darkness, of the black soul. Homage to thee for thy dark design. Thy servant awaits thy divine presence, that she may live again in the world of mortals…'"

Again the sigh echoed around the room. Adeline shivered. The temperature plummeted. Their breath clouded in front of them.

"I don't think I can stay down here, Professor."

"One more minute. Let me read this portion and then we will go up to the doctor's room—unless there is another way into that other basement."

Adeline glanced quickly around but the shadowy gloom didn't reveal any obvious entrances.

"'Set, my protector, redeem my soul. Free my spirit to live again. Let me see justice done and the manner of my death avenged.'" The professor moved back. "The late doctor was nothing if not faithful in his transcriptions."

"You believe the doctor wrote this? But how? When?"

"If not, who else?"

Adeline shook her head. "All I know is that this wall was bare when I last saw it."

"Then someone has been very busy." The professor continued to stare at the inscription. "I believe this is a copy of something he found in the scroll. It's a kind of spell. He really should have known better."

"In what way?"

"This has confirmed at least one of my suspicions. He was trying to get Cleopatra back. Not her body. No, that would continue to lie undisturbed and moldering in its tomb. He believed he could somehow transport her essence—her *ka* if you will—back here, to be born again in some host body of his choosing."

"You mean the girl who modeled for the portrait?"

"Possibly. Where is it, by the way?"

Adeline shone her lamp farther along the wall. Once again, that enigmatic face, reflected in the lamplight.

The professor hobbled over to it and reached up. "You told me Herr Klimt said there was something unnatural about it. If you steady me, Adeline, I believe I can get it down. We must examine it more closely."

Shock coursed through Adeline's veins. "I'm not sure that's wise, Professor." But Jakob Mayer was already balancing precariously on tiptoe. His fingertips touched the portrait, almost dislodging it. Adeline dashed over. She set the lamp on the floor and gripped the professor around the waist.

"Got it." A strong note of triumph resonated in his voice.

Another sigh, louder, more urgent, bounced off the walls.

"Shine your lamp closer so I can see."

Adeline did so. Close up, the full magnificence of the gold leaf, and that enigmatic profiled face were revealed as never before.

"Your Herr Klimt has done a truly inspiring job," the professor said. "Come on, we shall take this with us." He tucked the small portrait under his arm."

"I really don't think—"

"Nonsense, my dear. It's only a painting. You even know the artist."

"And he couldn't wait to get it out of his house."

"Nevertheless, we shall see it much clearer in daylight."

The professor had already started down the dark corridor. Adeline hurried after him. "I really should go ahead of you to make sure you don't trip in the dark. It's pitch black down here."

The professor stopped and let her pass, before urging her on. "Let's get a move on. We don't have all day and we still have a lot to do."

Adeline hurried as fast as her long skirt would permit her. She took the painting from the professor and clamped it under the arm that held the lamp, hoping she didn't drop it. They both made it into the library when a sudden gust of foul wind slammed the door shut.

Professor Mayer and Adeline stared at each other.

"Someone is most displeased with us," the professor said. He retrieved the painting.

"How can you be so calm, Professor? I'm scared witless. And you told me yesterday that I had been selected. For what? I never even met the man."

"Far too early to tell," the professor said, as he admired the painting, a small smile on his face. "This really is most fine. Most fine indeed. And you say Herr Klimt mixed some powder with the paint?"

"Yes, Dr. Quintillus insisted on that."

"I find that most interesting."

"But what does it mean, Professor? Was he mad? A deranged genius of some kind?"

"Quite possibly, but he knew his stuff and he had dabbled a lot in the old wisdom and magic of the ancient Egyptians. We can dismiss most of it with our scientific knowledge and discoveries since those far off days, but there are still elements of mysticism that even the esteemed Sherlock Holmes might find hard to debunk."

"I only wish I had never heard of Emeryk Quintillus. If I ever make it back to Wimbledon, I swear I shall never leave. However much money Miss Sinclair offers me."

"My dear girl, of course you will return to Wimbledon. We just have to crack this particular code. That's why I'm here. Please do not fret yourself any longer." He set the painting down on the desk. Adeline found she couldn't look at it anymore. It seemed too alive. Too real.

The professor hobbled across the library. "Come along now. Show me this man's room and let's see what we can find there."

———

They neared Dr. Quintillus's room. The dreaded smell of lilies hit them. Inside, Adeline heaved at the stench.

"How strange," the professor said, looking around the room. "I cannot understand where that smell is coming from."

"I can." Adeline pointed to a bowl of lilies on the floor, half hidden by the heavy bed cover.

"Most peculiar. Who would do such a thing?"

Adeline shrugged. "The entrance to the basement is over here." She went over to the wall and found the catch. A blast of cold air hit them. Curiously, this time, no stench of decay accompanied it.

Adeline lit the kerosene lamp and took the lead. As they entered the room, her skin crawled as if an army of ants was marching up and down her arms, neck, and back. No sound punctured the still, heavy gloom.

"This may sound crazy, Professor, but don't you think it's too quiet in here?"

The lamplight caught his nod. "I know exactly what you mean."

On the wall in front of them, something moved. Shimmered. A black shape took form. At first indistinct. Then…

"Professor! There's something in here with us!"

Professor Mayer stood, transfixed by the emerging figure in shadow on the wall. The body of a man with a jackal-like head and long, rectangular ears. Adeline dared to look over her shoulder. The lamp picked up no one but themselves.

"Set," the professor whispered. "But it's impossible." He looked around. "We are alone, but not alone. Extraordinary."

The figure on the wall raised its hand. With horror, Adeline realized what it intended to do.

"Professor!"

The god was a shadow no longer. It towered over them and took a menacing step closer to the professor, who seemed frozen to the spot.

"Professor!" Adeline called again. "It's going to strike you!"

Professor Mayer raised his arms to protect his head. "I'm unable to move. Something is preventing me."

Adeline tried to lift her foot. If she could just get over to him, pull him away, out of Set's reach, but her feet remained rooted to the floor.

The god raised the arm that held the staff.

"Leave him," Adeline cried. "He's an old man. He's no threat to you."

The god let out a mighty roar that echoed off the walls. Its arm sliced down and, with a sickening crack, the staff bounced off Professor Mayer's head. He let out a cry and crumpled, unconscious, to the floor.

The god's eyes flashed crimson, and it vanished.

Now freed from her paralysis, Adeline raced over to the injured professor

She set the lamp down on the floor and crouched down next to Professor Mayer. Her hands shook. She felt his neck for a pulse. Relief shot through her when she found one. "Thank God. I thought it had killed you for sure."

Jakob Mayer stirred and his eyes flickered open. He struggled to sit up, clutching his head. "It hurts like the very devil. Please help me up, my dear."

Adeline took his hands and heaved him to his feet. The professor staggered a little and leaned on Adeline. He put his hand back to his head. "If that hadn't just happened to me, I never would have believed it. Somehow the late Dr. Quintillus stirred up some ancient devils when he robbed the queen's tomb."

"Robbed it? You mean the dust he took, that he told Herr Klimt to use in the painting?"

"Oh, I think he took far more than that. Maybe he will tell us in his manuscript. You said he was about to enter the tomb in the last pages you typed?"

"Yes."

"I shall stay in Vienna all this week. In fact I shall stay here until we can lay the demons he raised. Now, though, I think we should get out of here."

Adeline was in no mood to argue.

Back in the doctor's room, the professor sat on the edge of the bed while Adeline searched under it and in any other place she thought she might have missed. The stench of lilies and the feeling they were being watched spurred her on to complete her task within minutes. She found nothing.

"At least I know I haven't missed anything here. Wherever Dr. Quintillus secreted that scroll, it certainly wasn't in this room."

The professor leaned heavily on his stick. After his ordeal he looked every one of his seventy-plus years.

"Oh, Professor, you have a red mark down the side of your face."

Professor Mayer touched his face and winced. "Here I presume? That creature certainly gave me a good hiding."

Adeline nodded, admiring the way Professor Mayer could still attempt levity, even in a situation like this.

He sighed and gave her a wry smile. "It seems in this house the impossible becomes reality a little too frequently."

"Come on, Professor, let's go back down to the library. It's probably those awful lilies, but this room is beginning to overpower me."

Back in the library, the fire crackled in the hearth, the room smelled pleasantly of polish, and Adeline could hardly believe the transformation that could take place at night when this comfortable place could scare her half out of her wits. Outside, the rain lashed on the windows and the sky hung heavy with storm clouds.

"I'll ask Magda to bring us some tea." Adeline tugged the bell-pull. The maid arrived almost immediately. If she saw the professor's injury she gave no reaction, but he faced away from her, so perhaps she didn't see. Adeline ordered their tea and the girl left.

"My dear," the professor said, "please bring that portrait over to me so I can examine it."

Adeline looked over at the desk. "It's not there!" She checked underneath. "It's disappeared. Maybe Magda… But I can't think why."

"Are you sure the portrait isn't there? Maybe I didn't leave it on the desk. My memory fails me sometimes these days."

"Oh, no, you definitely left it there. I watched you."

Magda brought in a tray with their tea.

"Magda," Adeline said, "did you come in earlier and notice a picture on the desk here?"

"A picture, madam? No. Apart from when you ordered tea, the last time I came in here was when I showed the professor in. I suppose one might have been there then, but I didn't notice."

"And Butters has been out since lunchtime?"

"Yes, madam. He and Frau Lederer went off to the Prater together at around eleven." Magda blushed and put a hand to her mouth, but Adeline wasn't in the least interested about any extra-curricular affairs the butler and the cook might be conducting. Or the fact Butters had lied to her about being out on important business.

"You are certain no one else has been in here today. No one but Professor Mayer has called?"

Magda shook her head.

"One more question, if I may. Did you place a bowl of lilies in Dr. Quintillus's room?"

The maid's eyes shot open. "No, madam. I never go in there. Mr. Butters told me I am not required to do anything on that floor. All the rooms are shut up."

Not quite all, Adeline thought. "Have you seen any lilies around in the last few days? Perhaps Butters brought some in."

Magda shook her head. "Mr. Butters doesn't like lilies. He told me they remind him of his mother's funeral. She died when he was very young, you see. He hasn't been able to stand the smell or even the sight of them ever since."

Adeline stared at the maid long and hard, searching for any sign the girl was lying, but could find none. Magda didn't strike her as a good enough actress to carry off any elaborate deception, and Adeline was as sure as she could be of her honesty. Call it a gut feeling. Whatever explanation existed for the missing picture, they could rule out theft by the maid.

After she had gone, Adeline poured tea and handed the professor a cup. It rattled against the saucer in her trembling hands.

"Thank you, my dear. Now sit down and let us examine this rationally."

Adeline brought her tea and sat in a chair opposite the professor. She gave a little start and pointed to his face. "Professor, the red mark has disappeared. But how could it have gone so quickly?."

Professor Mayer touched his face. "It doesn't hurt now and nor does my head. Something is playing with us, trying to make us believe we are losing our reason." He raised his voice. "It will not succeed."

"Professor, do you believe that Dr. Quintillus is somewhere in this house, either dead or somehow alive? Did I really see him, or was that an illusion?"

"I truly do not know. I think most of those alternatives are possible because there are dark forces here. Ancient forces that have been disturbed and are showing their displeasure. I think it most unlikely he is still alive in any sense that we would accept in the natural order of things, and I do believe that the painting is possessed in some way. It has the ability to relocate, but I have no idea how. This is not my field of expertise. I am an historian. An Egyptologist. I do my best to debunk any notions of ancient curses and mysticism, but I must confess that, within a few minutes of entering that basement, I began to doubt the convictions I have held for a lifetime. I need to do some research. When

I have some news for you, I shall get word to you to meet me. You can go out in the evenings, I presume?"

"I haven't done so yet, but there is no reason why I couldn't."

"Good."

"Please address anything to me in a sealed envelope. I have an uneasy relationship with the butler and, despite what Magda said, I can't help but wonder if he is responsible for the lilies in Dr. Quintillus's room. The man retains his loyalty to his deceased master."

"I will be sure and do that. I shall even seal the envelope with my own personal wax seal. That way you can be sure he will not tamper with it."

"Thank you, Professor. I hope I haven't put you in danger. After what happened today…"

"Don't worry yourself, my dear. I have taken care of myself for a great many years. I am sure I can continue to do so for a few more yet."

———

The next morning, when Adeline returned to the library, she gasped. Next to her typewriter lay the picture, exactly where the professor had placed it the previous day. She heard a noise coming from the hall. Butters. She quickly obscured the portrait with some sheets of typing paper. The butler brought in her breakfast, his mouth turned down at the corners. He avoided her gaze. It had become almost a game. Adeline trying to force him to look her in the eyes and Butters steadfast in his determination not to.

"Thank you," she said. He didn't reply, turned and left her alone.

Adeline swept the paper away and stared at the portrait. *Where did you wander off to yesterday, and how did you get back?*

On a sudden impulse, Adeline touched the face. The paint felt oddly grainy under her fingers. Cold, unpleasantly moist. She turned her hand over to stare at her fingers. They seemed coated in a fine gray powder. Dry. Not moist at all. Yet, when she had carried the picture under her arm from the basement, she had been unaware of any residue on her clothes. Trepidation seeped from every pore of her being but she raised her fingers to sniff them. A disgusting odor of mold, decay and the stench of a long dead animal, like a mouse she had found once behind a kitchen cupboard.

She gagged and ran out of the library, leaving the picture exposed on the desk.

She was already washing her hands in the bathroom when she remembered she had left the portrait right where anyone entering the library would be sure to see it. She raced downstairs again. Relief. Her uneaten breakfast, and the picture were still there.

She opened a drawer in the desk and used the tray cloth to avoid contact with the portrait. She quickly shoved it away and closed the drawer.

When Butters returned five minutes later, he found her finishing a slice of toast.

He laid her day's work down by her typewriter, without a word, and removed her breakfast tray. She thanked him again. He merely nodded, almost imperceptibly.

> Words cannot express here my emotions on beholding the face of my beloved queen. The state of preservation was far better than others I have witnessed, but even though an artist's imagination would be needed to picture her as she once was, I still felt her beauty and her power over all hearts, both male and female. To know that soon her spirit would greet me was overpowering. I bent to kiss her cold, dry lips, and my heart soared...

Adeline typed the words and marveled at how this academic—normally cold and dry as his beloved's lips—had suddenly been swept up in a passion to equal that of any romantic novel.

But the next paragraph brought her up sharp.

> I saw the glint of gold and there it was. Precisely as the scroll had said it would be. Clutched in her hand. She clung to it in death as she had in life, but finally gave it up to me and I held it in my hands. The statue of Set. It felt cold to my touch and then warmed, as if being

revitalized by my life force. So much power in one little statue. The power of life over death. Unseen by Dressler, who was too busy mopping up his sweat, I tucked the statuette in my pocket. It lies there still. Never leaving my person for fear it should fall into the wrong hands...

Adeline stopped typing. That statue. It had to be still here in this house and, if so, maybe it was in Quintillus's pocket. After all, he had been wearing a long jacket when she had seen him in the basement. Assuming it really *was* him. She had to tell the professor, but the butler mustn't know. At lunchtime she would scribble a note and mail it to Professor Mayer at the hotel. If the local Vienna mail was anything like London, he should receive it by later that afternoon or early evening. Tomorrow at the latest.

She resumed her work, excitement mounting inside her.

I had one more task to perform. The wrappings that bound her body were worn away in part and I was able to insert my fingers underneath them. Touching my beloved's breast, I could swear I felt her heart beat once under my hand. I took out the little bag I had brought with me and scooped up a small handful of fine ash. I poured this carefully into the bag and returned a few times more, making sure I had collected enough for my purpose. Now I had what I needed. I could stay no longer. Every minute could risk exposure of my discovery. Reluctantly, I left her, consoling myself with the knowledge that I was merely leaving her earthly body from another age. I carried her spirit with me. Still resolved that none should set eyes on her, I put my plan in operation. Dressler is a fool. He suspects nothing. How the museum could entrust such a valuable project to such an imbecile defeats me. He will be no loss to the world or to antiquity...

With increasing horror, Adeline typed the cold account of how Dr. Quintillus buried all who had witnessed the greatest discovery of the century and more. Alive. He had shot Dressler as if he had stamped on a troublesome insect. Then he had calmly ridden away, back to Alexandria and the ship that would take him to Italy and thence home to Vienna.

After a hastily eaten lunch, Adeline wrote her quick note to the professor and hurried out to mail it. When she returned, gloom hung over the library. And it didn't just come from the dreary afternoon. She switched on the electric light and tried to ignore the sense of dread that infected her pores. At her desk, she remembered the portrait sitting in that drawer. She shook her head and concentrated on her typing. The rest of the pages recounted the self-satisfied triumph of a man who had achieved his ambition at the expense of others. It sickened Adeline to the core.

After dinner, Adeline didn't go immediately to her room as had become her habit. She had finished her book and wanted to choose another, so she made her way up the spiral staircase to the collection of English novels. She became engrossed in searching through the titles when she realized the room was growing darker. She looked up. The lights were still on, but they seemed dimmer somehow. Adeline knew nothing about how electricity worked. Could the lights dim like that? Perhaps the bulbs needed changing.

She shrugged and carried on, searching along the shelves, alighting on Charlotte Bronte's *Jane Eyre*. She had read it many years earlier and enjoyed it but, on flicking through the pages to remind herself of the story, she decided that a dark mystery was perhaps not the most reassuring for someone in her current position. She reached up to replace the book on the shelves when the lights went out.

Plunged into darkness, Adeline froze. A strange greenish light began as a flickering shadow of a candle flame, reflecting against the bookshelves down below her, behind the desk. Not three feet from where the portrait lay. The light grew, glowing and pulsing. Adeline watched, too terrified to move and unable to see her way.

A crash. Something fell down behind the desk. The eerie light stopped pulsing, brightened, waned and died away. The electric lights came up and grew stronger. Adeline let out her breath and continued to stare over at the desk.

Only when she was as sure as she could be that it was all over, did she dare to descend.

She crept across the room, anxious not to make a sound in case she would disturb anything that might be lying dormant. Behind the desk lay an upturned drawer on the floor. Adeline bent to retrieve it. Empty. No sign of the painting. Adeline prayed she wouldn't see it on her bedroom wall that night.

She didn't. But she hardly slept. The long night dragged on. The house stayed silent. No more noises from downstairs. Standing by the window, she watched the sun come up on a cold, pinky-gray dawn and wished she were back in Wimbledon. A wave of homesickness brought tears to her eyes. Maybe she would leave here after all. After all, there were other agencies. But they would want references from Miss Sinclair and, at this moment, Adeline wasn't at all sure she would get one under such circumstances. Whichever way she looked at it, the same likely outcome presented itself. She would render herself unemployable and where would that leave her? The prospect didn't bear thinking about. No. She would have to "toughen up and sweat it out" as James used to say whenever faced with some unpleasant prospect.

With a sigh, she turned back into the room and began to prepare herself for another day.

She was dressed and in the bathroom, brushing her teeth, when the footsteps sounded. Light at first, then rapidly building to a crescendo, they thundered closer along the corridor. The locked bathroom door rattled, faster and faster.

It stopped. Adeline gripped the sink hard and prayed. *Make it go away. Whatever it is, make it go away.* Green light flashed through the keyhole. A long, low moan became a whistling wind blowing its foul stench of death through that same keyhole. Adeline backed away to the far wall, holding her nose against the smell. It blew through her hair, infected her clothes.

A wave of anger momentarily took hold of her fear. "Stop this! Go back to hell where you belong!" She did not know where that had come from, only that it was her voice and her emotions.

The green light snapped off, and the howling wind stopped. The lock clicked as if someone had released it on the outside, but she was staring at the unmoving key on the *inside*. The door swung gently open.

Adeline edged out into the corridor. She looked up and down. Nothing. No sign that anyone had been there. Just her.

She crept back to her bedroom and took a deep breath before she turned the handle. Once inside, her gaze went immediately to the wall above the mantelpiece.

She gasped.

The portrait was back.

Chapter 7

In the Café Central, Professor Mayer mopped the corners of his mouth with his table napkin and leaned forward. Adeline moved in closer so he could keep his voice low.

"Especially after what you've now told me, I believe it is imperative we find the late doctor's scroll as quickly as we can. I also believe it is vital we find that gold statuette. Once we have them, I believe we are in a much stronger position to proceed with undoing the evil that he has unleashed."

Adeline blinked. "Surely we need to destroy the portrait as well."

"No, Adeline. That is the very last thing we should do."

"But I'm sure it's responsible for so much that's going on. The woman's voice, the scratching in the walls and the thumps. That green light I told you about. And the way it keeps moving and turning up on my bedroom wall."

"It's not still there?"

Adeline shook her head. "By the time I dared to return to my room, in the evening, it had gone. But every time I go in there, I feel sure I'm going to see it again."

Professor Mayer clasped Adeline's hand, which she had unconsciously balled into a fist. "My dear girl, you must calm yourself or you will make yourself ill. Please trust me. We need to return to that cellar—to the room where you saw the body of Dr. Quintillus. We must take more lamps with us and search thoroughly. I'm sure we've missed something."

Adeline's eyes widened. The mere thought of returning to that awful place filled her with dread. She would rather have run naked around Vienna's Ringstrasse than go back down there. Even with the professor.

"Professor, I can't..."

Professor Mayer squeezed her hand. "Yes, you can. And you will. There really isn't an alternative option."

She stared at him, trying to think of one. Without success. She had finally admitted to herself that her presence in that house was no mere coincidence. Emeryk Quintillus had targeted her, although for what purpose she hadn't any idea. Now she must see it through.

She gritted her teeth. "Saturday then." Today was only Tuesday. "If I can bear to stay that long."

"I urge you most strongly not to think of leaving. Whatever has been unleashed will merely come after you. If I'm right, and I believe I am, you would probably arrive home to find that accursed portrait on a wall in your house and you really don't want ancient wrath of this kind in your own home."

"But there's something I really don't understand. Dr. Quintillus was besotted with Cleopatra. He wanted her for himself. He loved her. He would be her willing slave. Why would she be so angry with him?"

"Simple. Quintillus may have been besotted with her, but why should she reciprocate? She chose to die the way she did, in order to be with her beloved Mark Antony. Her body still is. Albeit, according to the late doctor, not as close by as she would have desired. Dr. Quintillus, in removing that gold statuette, also removed her spirit, which—it would appear—was being guarded by the god of death, Set. By his actions, the doctor angered a powerful queen and an even more powerful deity. He may also have disturbed another unquiet spirit and released yet more danger that should have remained incarcerated at Taposiris Magna. It is my belief that he brought the wrath of these ancient ones down on himself. I believe that, ultimately, it cost him his life."

"So...they killed him? But where is his body? In the house, mummified as I saw it?"

Professor Mayer let go Adeline's hand, leaned back and took a deep breath. He appeared to consider her question for a moment before he exhaled. "To the first question, I would say yes, most assuredly. As to your last two questions, I am afraid I don't know. Nor have I yet worked out the real purpose of the painting, although I would guess by including the dust from her sarcophagus, he meant to recreate her in some way."

"But what about the model? Wasn't she Cleopatra? Hadn't he already brought her back from the dead?" Adeline put her hand to her head; a sharp headache thumped at her temples. She took a few sips from the glass of water that always accompanied coffee in Vienna.

"I don't understand that myself. No doubt more will be revealed as you move further into your assignment. As we've seen, Dr. Quintillus seems at great pains to cover every last detail. The problem is, the way things are progressing, we simply haven't the time to wait and see. That is why we must find that scroll. I believe many of the answers will lie there."

"It's so infuriating that I only receive the manuscript piecemeal."

"I share your frustration, my dear, but we must be patient a little longer. I'm also in contact with some of my former colleagues at Oxford. Not a day goes by here that I don't thank Mr. Alexander Graham Bell for his marvelous invention." He smiled.

Tomorrow I shall be back in Vienna. The overnight train journey was not without curious incident. As I lay, trying to sleep in the impossible heat of my stuffy compartment, I imagined I saw a faint green light in one corner. It seemed to emanate from my jacket. I rose from my bed and reached into the pocket. Instantly, the green light winked off. I pulled out the statue of Set and turned it over in my hand. I never fail to marvel at the power that surges through my veins every time I touch it. My heart beats a little quicker, and I feel closer to my beloved…

Adeline rested her hands on the desk and scanned the remaining ten pages. Not once did he mention the scroll, and today's work was more concerned with his journey back, meetings with various academics at Vienna University and his delight at the ceiling of his library.

Herr Klimt has done excellent work. I believe I shall have a most important commission for him very soon.

Infuriatingly, he said no more about it then, nor on any of the sheets Butters handed her over the next two days. In fact, Dr. Quintillus seemed more concerned with the so-called "gypsy scourge" and the rantings of a painter called Adolf Hitler. From what she read, it seemed the archeologist favored repatriating gypsy families who, he believed, were nothing but thieves, wastrels, and prostitutes. Yet again, she thanked providence she had never met the man whose manuscript she was typing so meticulously.

Professor Mayer arrived early on Saturday morning, complete with a Gladstone bag of generous proportions, which he set down by the desk. He seemed energized and didn't move as stiffly as on the last time she had seen him. Magda had earlier ensured a crackling fire warmed the library. The professor advanced toward it, and Adeline held his walking stick while he warmed his chilled hands.

"It's snowing heavens' hard out there. This winter doesn't want to let go its grip, does it?"

"No, indeed, Professor. It's very slippery underfoot as well. I hope you take care when you're out and about."

"Of course my dear." He rubbed his hands together one last time and retrieved his stick from Adeline's outstretched hand. "Let us proceed. Up to the late doctor's bedroom I believe. Best to bring that lamp along as well this time if we are to have a good chance of seeing whatever needs to be seen in that basement."

Adeline picked up the table lamp and, having made sure Magda wasn't around to see them, she and the professor made their silent way up the stairs and along the corridor.

Quintillus's room was quiet and no longer reeked of lilies. On checking the side of the bed, Adeline saw the bowl had been removed.

The professor picked up the other lamp and lit it while Adeline lit hers.

"I'd better carry them both," she said.

"Not at all, my dear. I can manage perfectly well. I shall hook my walking stick over my arm and lean on the handrail. Now I am familiar with these steps, I shall be perfectly safe."

Adeline felt relieved she, too, would have a hand free to steady herself on the way down. She always had a sensation of something following her. Something that might welcome an opportunity to throw her off balance and send her crashing to the stone floor below.

At the foot of the steps, the atmosphere seemed to close in on Adeline. An unwelcome cloak that threatened to suffocate her. The professor turned. "You feel it, too?"

She nodded.

"Come along, my dear. Let's find what we came for."

Once inside, light from both lamps illuminated the detail of the mostly empty room more clearly.

The professor peered at the far wall. He moved closer to inspect it. "I think I may have found another entrance."

Adeline hurried to join him and shone her lamp next to his. She could just make out the outline of a concealed doorway, similar to that in Quintillus's room. The professor was already feeling his way down the left-hand side to find a catch. A click. The door swung open. A familiar fusty smell of stale air and dust greeted them.

The professor touched her arm. "Let's see where this takes us."

Adeline's heartbeat thumped in her ears. She followed the professor inside. Yet another room.

"I should imagine the entire basement is a network of interconnecting rooms." Professor Mayer said. "Let's see what this one has to offer and if we can find another entrance. Perhaps one that will lead us into the room with the portrait."

Something small and black scurried across the floor. Its carapace was curiously iridescent.

"Just a beetle," the professor said. "And from my brief glimpse, I wouldn't be at all surprised to find it was of the scarab variety."

Adeline's voice quivered. "It looked like the one I saw in the fire that evening."

The professor nodded. "Interesting."

Adeline tried to reassure herself. "Old houses and beetles go together. I'm sure it doesn't mean anything."

She studied the professor's expression. "If you say so, my dear. I'm sure you're right."

Adeline wasn't reassured. A breath of foul air tickled the hairs on the back of her neck. She clutched the professor's arm. "There's something down here with us. Can you smell that? Did you feel it?"

"Yes, my dear. It means we're getting close."

Adeline marveled at how calm he sounded, while all she wanted to do was pick up her skirt and run.

Her lamp flickered, then grew stronger again. The windowless room held some broken furniture and old wine cases.

A green luminescence began to form on the wall opposite them.

"This is the light you've seen before, I take it." Professor Mayer said, moving closer.

"Yes. Oh, Professor, I wouldn't go anywhere near it."

The glow began to pulsate and then shimmer. A shadow took form on the wall. The jackal head on the man's body.

Adeline called out. "Professor, do take care! Remember what it did to you last time!"

Professor Mayer backed away and rejoined Adeline. A hunched figure emerged as the shadows retreated. A familiar one in a tall stovepipe hat, long hair fanning its shoulders.

"Dr. Quintillus," Adeline whispered, gripping the professor's arm.

The figure grew in substance, while the shadow of Set faded, along with the glow. In profile, the late doctor sat on a chair, his head bent forward. His hair and beard concealed his face. Death, decay, rot, and a saltiness that reminded Adeline of contaminated sea water in a stagnant pool flooded the room.

Adeline remained rooted to the spot, but the professor took a few steps forward. While she watched, horrified, he reached out his hand and touched the figure on the shoulder.

"This is no ghost," he said.

Adeline held her breath while the professor moved slowly around to the front and, with his thumb and forefinger, lifted the head.

A rustling, crackling sound echoed through the room. Adeline flinched as, without warning, and of its own accord, the head of Dr. Quintillus turned and stared at her, with its eyeless, mummified face.

"It's all right, Adeline. The doctor is most assuredly dead."

Adeline couldn't take her eyes off the blank expression, made all the worse by those two, eyeless black holes.

"But he moved his head," she said.

"You may have seen that, but I didn't."

"Professor, his head turned. He's staring at me."

"We are seeing different things, my dear. Tell me, do you smell anything? Lilies perhaps?"

The sickening odor reached Adeline's nose and she wrinkled it in disgust. "Yes. It's overpowering."

"This time I do not. You alone are meant to smell it, because lilies represent death to you."

"I don't understand."

"No, my dear, neither do I. But I believe it is a far from subtle way of communicating to you that you have been selected for some purpose. Something to do with the afterlife, but any more than that I haven't any idea." The professor removed his thumb and forefinger and Quintillus's head crackled like dead leaves as it dropped down onto his chest.

"How did he get here?" Adeline asked.

The professor shook his head. "I can only guess he has been here all the time."

"But we saw him appear. He wasn't here when we came in. And last time he was in a different room. The first one we came through."

The professor was concentrating on the wall behind the corpse. "That would be pretty easy to accomplish. These concealed entrances make physical movement all too straightforward. I would imagine also, that we may well recognize the room on the other side of this." He pressed the wall. A click. A cold draft ruffled Adeline's hair.

Professor Mayer nodded. "Before we go inside, I want to check something."

Adeline watched in horror. The professor reached his hand into first one and then the other outer pocket of the late doctor's jacket. He shook his head and reached into the inner pockets.

Adeline breathed a sigh of relief when he withdrew his empty hand.

"No, that would have been too easy. They don't want us to find it yet. If ever. But we shall."

The queen and the god? This other unquiet spirit he had mentioned? Whoever was orchestrating this, someone was working her like a puppet, dangling on a piece of string. Resentment and anger rolled up in a tight wad in Adeline's stomach and began to reach upward. These might be forces she knew little about, but she would be damned if she would let them take her over.

"Let us proceed, my dear." The professor didn't wait for her response. He was already making his way around the body and into the next room.

Adeline gave Quintillus's mummified body as wide a berth as possible, but the rotten stench sent bile rushing up into her throat. She swallowed it down and gritted her teeth.

"As I suspected." The professor held his lamp up high on the wall. They had returned to the room with the hieroglyphics and the portrait was back on the wall.

Behind Adeline came a soft, whooshing sound. She spun around in time to see the door swinging shut, but at least in here they had an alternative route out. She shone her lamp around until she caught the welcome sight of the exit, leading to the corridor and steps to the library.

"Let's have a proper look around this room," Professor Mayer said.

Adeline joined him and their combined lamps lit up the dark corners. A small, black chest of drawers she had somehow failed to notice before reflected in the light.

"Ah, that looks promising." Professor Mayer set his lamp down on the top of the small chest and tugged at the top drawer. It gave without too much effort.

Adeline concentrated on remaining calm and illuminating his efforts with her lamp.

"I have something." He pulled out a tightly rolled scroll and began to unravel it. A broad smile lit up his face.

"What is it, Professor?"

"I shall need to examine it and translate it but, if I'm not mistaken, we may have found the doctor's precious scroll."

Adeline didn't get a chance to speak. A loud crash sounded from the next room. A figure stood in the entrance. Tall. Male. In a long jacket and stovepipe hat.

The dead face reflected gray in the light.

Adeline licked dry lips. "Tell me you can see him standing there, Professor. Tell me I'm not the only one who can see that."

"Indeed you are not, Adeline," the professor said. "Good evening, Dr. Quintillus."

Chapter 8

The mummified figure stood motionless. Its rotten odor filled the room.

In Adeline's ear, a woman's voice she had heard before, whispered in its unintelligible language. Anger once again drowned her fear and poured out of her. "Speak in a language I understand or shut up!"

Professor Mayer's expression mingled shock with amusement.

Adeline couldn't believe what she had just said. Her cheeks burned. "Sorry, Professor. I wasn't referring to you. I keep hearing this woman whispering gibberish in my ear. I've had enough of her."

Professor Mayer nodded and addressed the silent figure in the doorway. "Dr. Quintillus, will you tell us what you have done with the statue you stole from Cleopatra's tomb? You will not rest until you make amends for this terrible crime."

Quintillus didn't move.

"Dr. Quintillus, I believe I have the scroll. I have the means and knowledge to translate it. Soon I hope to undo what you sought to do."

A cracking noise, like someone walking across eggshells.

"Professor! The portrait!"

It glowed in a shimmer of iridescent gold and green.

The profile slowly moved. Adeline watched in horrified fascination. "She's turning…"

"Intriguing," the professor said. He limped closer to peer at the picture. "Could you bring your lamp, my dear? I need to see this in a better light."

How could he remain so calm? Adeline could barely breathe.

The professor spoke gently, but firmly. "Come my dear, the lamp. Please."

Adeline cast a quick glance back over her shoulder. Relief. Quintillus had gone.

Reluctantly, she staggered over to join the professor. She stared at the haughty, regal face in the portrait. Its frozen gaze seemed to bare her soul. This would not be a woman you would want to cross—alive or dead. Adeline shivered in the sudden chill.

"Yes, I noticed the drop in temperature." Professor Mayer exhaled.

Adeline flinched from the palpable force of the portrait. The face— now staring straight at her—had taken on so much life. Both eyes bored into her brain. Images of pyramids, desert, and swaying palm trees played through her mind. Anger and sadness that she knew were not her own welled up inside her, threatening to spill over, along with an unquenchable thirst for revenge.

Professor Mayer must have sensed her disquiet. He laid his hand lightly on her arm, and she tore her gaze away from the hypnotic hold of the portrait.

"Come, my dear. Away from that now." He had tucked the scroll under his arm and now withdrew it. "Hold onto this, would you? I think we should return to the library. I must begin to translate this scroll."

Adeline forced herself to keep looking away from the picture, although it tugged at her, drawing her to it. She shook herself, trying to rid herself of its power. Another fear hit her. "What if Dr. Quintillus is waiting for us in the library?" She shivered again.

"Then we shall act accordingly," Professor Mayer said. He didn't elaborate.

———

The chill stayed with them. It crept along the corridor and back upstairs. Adeline made to enter the library. An icy gust knocked her off balance. Professor Mayer caught her.

"We have certainly drawn attention to ourselves."

Adeline grabbed the handle firmly this time. Freezing to the touch. "Maybe she didn't like me telling her to shut up. Whoever she is."

Back in the warmth of the library, Adeline breathed steadily, trying to slow her racing heartbeat. She set down the lamp and handed the scroll to the professor.

In daylight, the yellowing scroll looked ancient, worn and stained. Professor Mayer carefully unrolled it. He laid it down on the desk, placing paperweights and books to hold the corners flat. All four edges were torn and ragged, the bottom in worse condition than the others. Adeline leaned over. The handwritten script used an alphabet she didn't recognize.

The professor bent and peered closely at the cramped words. "Ancient Greek. Cleopatra and her family were of Greek descent, you know."

"Can you understand what it says?"

"I'm a little rusty, but yes. I should be able to translate this. It would appear to have been written by a contemporary of Mark Antony and Cleopatra's. Someone who took great pains to provide an accurate account of exactly where she was buried and also of the dire consequences for anyone who should attempt to separate her from her beloved."

"Do we know who wrote it? Is there a signature?"

The professor studied it carefully. "There doesn't appear to be. In any case, the writer of this wouldn't consider his name to be of any consequence. He—and it was almost undoubtedly a male—acted out of love and loyalty to his queen."

Professor Mayer removed the weights and rolled up the scroll, which he placed in his bag.

"Now I can see why you brought that," Adeline said.

Professor Mayer smiled. "I hoped I might find something to put in it today."

"But Professor, if we've angered whatever is down there sufficiently, aren't we in danger of ending up like Dr. Quintillus?"

"Not if I have anything to do with it. My dear Adeline, stay calm a little longer. I am convinced that the answers lie in this scroll, which I will begin work on as soon as I return to the hotel. If I run into difficulties, I can always use their telephone to talk to one of my former colleagues. Please try not to worry. I will meet you tomorrow at six thirty in the lobby of my hotel. We shall have some dinner in their excellent restaurant and I shall report my progress. In the meantime, I suggest you stay out of this room except when you're working, and on no account venture down into the basement or up to the late doctor's room."

"I can assure you I have no intention of doing either of those things. And I will take your advice about this room."

Not that it would stop the picture from manifesting itself on her bedroom wall. Adeline tried to put that thought out of her mind.

———

That night, she slept better and woke refreshed for once. The strange events of the previous day seemed impossible. If she had been alone, she could have probably convinced herself she had imagined or dreamed them.

She glanced at the wall and breathed a sigh of relief. No picture. She washed and dressed and went down in time to see Butters crossing the hall with her breakfast tray in his hands.

"Good morning, Butters," she said.

He stopped and turned. "Good morning, madam."

Still the disdainful formality. Adeline chose to ignore it.

Butters laid the tray in front of her.

"Did you have an enjoyable day off yesterday?" she asked. Butters seemed taken aback. He obviously hadn't expected to be asked such a question.

"Yes, madam."

"Good." Adeline had begun to wonder if he had heard her. His expression had changed. His eyes were wide and staring at a point over and behind her head. His complexion blanched.

Adeline turned her head to follow his gaze. She jumped out of her chair at the sight of the green incandescence, barely perceptible, but clearly pulsating. She moved round the desk.

"How often have you seen that, Butters?"

The strange glow vanished. The butler drew himself together. "Seen what, madam?"

"That green light."

"I saw nothing, madam."

Adeline went back to her side of the desk and faced the butler. Anger coiled cobra-like in her stomach. "Why are you lying? You saw that green glow as clearly as I did. Now, how many times have you seen it before?"

"I don't know to what you are referring, madam. If you'll excuse me, I have work to do."

He left her alone. Adeline chewed her lip. That butler knew far more than he was prepared to reveal, and he was easily as scared as she was. That might prove useful.

———

A few days later, Professor Mayer was waiting for her in the lobby of his hotel, a glass of Madeira in front of him and a black notebook placed next to it. Adeline sat down opposite him.

"How are you getting on with the scroll?" she asked.

"Very well. Better than I thought. It's funny how it all comes back to you. Even though I believed I'd forgotten so much classical Greek, as soon as I began, the words started to return, and I have completed almost half of it."

"And what have you learned?"

"That the late doctor should have taken heed of the entire contents of the scroll and not only the parts that led him to Cleopatra's tomb. The scroll says that Cleopatra was buried clutching the gold statue of Set to protect her in the afterlife and keep her spirit close to Mark Antony's. Should the statue be removed, her spirit would accompany it. This much I already gathered, but what I didn't know until now was the precise nature of the dire warnings of what would happen to anyone removing that statue. These are the warnings the late doctor chose to ignore, at his peril. I, on the other hand, am inclined to give them credence. Especially after what we saw in the basement."

"What was the curse? That Dr. Quintillus would be killed?"

"Not just killed. The curse read that anyone removing the statue from the tomb would suffer death from every drop of liquid being drained from the body. All that would remain of them would be a dry husk, doomed to walk the place of their incarceration. In Dr. Quintillus's case, that, I believe, is the basement of his own house."

"But he didn't die until two years after he stole the statue. He even had chance to write his memoirs. And what about the portrait?"

"I was coming to that. As for the time delay, it is not uncommon, in legend at least, to read of such a curse not being enacted for months or even years after the event which has precipitated it. It's like a ticking clock, attached to a bomb. Only the one who issued the curse knows when it will go off. As for the portrait, the scroll describes the potency of the mummy of the deceased queen. Dr. Quintillus must have deduced that, by using the dust in the creation of the painting, he would be able to make Cleopatra live again."

"And the model for the portrait?"

Professor Mayer shook his head. "I have no idea. The scroll doesn't mention that. At least not yet. I should imagine he searched for someone who looked a lot like her. Maybe he even brought her back with him from Egypt, although I'm assuming he didn't mention this."

"No."

"Then that at least will have to remain a mystery. For the moment, at any rate. The scroll also hints at the great age of the statue. It says it was blessed by the god himself. I cannot possibly pass judgment on that."

The professor leaned on his stick to hoist himself to his feet. Adeline assisted him.

"Thank you, my dear. Let's go and eat. I am famished. They do an excellent pike-perch here. Have you ever eaten *Zanderfilet*?"

Adeline shook her head.

"It's often called pike-perch because it has characteristics of both fish. A delicious local specialty."

Frau Lederer's dishes were always tasty and well-cooked, but tonight Adeline felt pampered, even to the extent of a glass of chilled, white wine. It lifted her spirits and managed to dampen down some of the raw edges of her apprehension.

After the dishes had been cleared, Professor Mayer leaned closer. The restaurant was almost full, with plenty of chatter to drown out their conversation.

"Now I come to the difficult part of my discoveries today."

Adeline inhaled deeply.

"By the way you're talking, would I be right in guessing this is the part that concerns me?"

"Yes, my dear, I'm afraid you would, if my deductions are correct and, of course, there is always the possibility they may not be."

But Adeline knew the professor well enough to know that if he had even the slightest doubt of his facts, he wouldn't mention them to her. She steeled herself.

"The scroll says that most of Cleopatra's children were raised in Rome by Octavia, who had been the first wife of Mark Antony. There was a set of twins—Alexander Helios and Cleopatra Selene—born out of the union between Cleopatra and Mark Antony. All of this is in recorded history, but the scroll goes onto state that, should the gold statue be removed and the curse be enacted, only one person will be able to set it right and that is a direct descendent of Cleopatra and Mark Antony. You once told me of the old legends in your family. That you were directly descended from Cleopatra."

"But that was fantasy. No one really believed it."

"I think you should begin to believe it, my dear, because proof will shortly be on its way from Oxford."

"How can there be proof? This happened two thousand years ago. No one can trace their family line back that far."

"You told me that your mother had been brought up believing she was descended from Cleopatra and Mark Antony. Her mother had told her, and her grandmother had passed on the legend to her. Why isn't it possible that each successive mother has told their children the same thing?"

Adeline's mind raced. "But even assuming for one moment that I am related to her, there must be thousands of us. It's not beyond the bounds of coincidence that Dr. Quintillus's lawyers would happen to choose one of us. We probably walk past relations every day, but we don't know them."

"Very true, my dear, but you see, there is a little more to it than that. I said proof of your genealogy was on its way and then you will see. My Oxford friend informed me that he had become convinced beyond all reasonable doubt that you are Cleopatra's descendant and it is most important for Dr. Quintillus that you should be."

"But why, Professor? I don't understand. He's dead. Killed by a curse he was responsible for triggering."

"Dead, yes, but not resting in peace. His spirit still longs for his beloved Cleopatra. To spend eternity with her. Only one person can make that happen. It has to be a direct descendant of Cleopatra herself. This is why you were chosen. My friend told me a firm of solicitors contacted him a year or so ago and asked him to research the descendants of Cleopatra and Mark Antony. He did so, spending many months on his painstaking work. Most of the lines petered out as yours will, should you not have children. This resulted in a surprising few. Around fifty are alive today, scattered all over the globe, anywhere from Russia to Africa and Asia. Most do not speak or write English. In the end, there were just two who did. One of those is in the United States and is elderly and infirm. That left you."

Adeline had listened, wide-eyed through all of this. "But supposing I hadn't been a typist?"

"That was their good fortune—or, should I say, the doctor's. However, I believe the manuscript is a ruse. Dr. Quintillus never expected it to be published. Indeed, it if it was, all would be lost. His beloved queen's final resting place would be revealed for all the world to visit and gawp at. It would be no time before her mummified corpse would be put on display at the British Museum or some such place."

Something else puzzled Adeline. "If the doctor was the only one still alive who knew the whereabouts of the scroll—and what it contained—who arranged for the lawyers to find me? If this happened a year or so ago, he was already dead."

"He may have known his fate before he died. Or, more likely, someone else acted out of loyalty. Someone in whom he may have confided."

"Butters?"

"Perhaps. You said he had a cook who still works there?"

"Frau Lederer, yes. Do you know, in all these weeks, I have never so much as laid eyes on her? She stays downstairs in her kitchen—"

"Downstairs you say?" The professor's eyes lit up.

"Yes." What a curious question.

"The kitchen would be at the same level as the basement then?"

"I suppose so, yes. Hopefully with a window or two though."

"And you have never been down there, or met her?"

Adeline shook her head.

"Then I would suggest it's high time you did. Make up some excuse. Say you wish to compliment her on her delicious food. Anything you like but get down there. Tomorrow if you can. I have a feeling what you learn may be of great interest to us. But do be careful."

"Oh, I will. Frankly, Professor, I'm far too scared not to be. I would give anything to be able to pack up my typewriter and leave Vienna forever." Adeline's eyes filled with tears. The professor laid a comforting hand over hers. "I'm sorry," she said, "All my life I longed to be able to visit the city my grandfather loved so much and for it to turn out like this... It's like my whole world has come crashing down on me again."

―――――

The next day, she started on the latest pages. By now, Dr. Quintillus had moved on to write about the planned portrait of Cleopatra.

> *My dilemma continues. To find the right model. The blend of striking looks and personality that will lift the picture off the canvas and make it live. In the hands of a master such as Herr Klimt, this will not be difficult, but a good artist must firstly have good material on which to exercise his supreme talent...*

Two pages on, success.

> *I have found her! She was so close, but I failed to realize the essence of her existence, her true nature, until my eyes were opened... Yet there is something disquieting about the way she looks at me. Although she is my ideal of Cleopatra, she seems, at times, removed*

from reality. I noticed it first when I showed her the statue of Set. She held it for a second and a tremor passed through her entire body. She looked at me as if seeing me for the first time and her eyes stared through me. Her gaze was almost one of contempt. She handed me back the statue and the moment ended, but still I wonder. Did something pass from the statue to the woman? She seems different since that day...

Adeline skipped through the rest of the day's pages, searching for more on the enigmatic woman, but not once did Quintillus offer a name, location or any other detail except constant references to the woman's beauty and queenly—if sometimes disturbing— presence.

I will take her each day to Herr Klimt's studio and I will wait for her. If I leave her alone with him for one second, I fear for the consequences, although not for the further extension of the artist's reputation as a womanizer. Rather, I am concerned about what she will do. She barely speaks to me these days and eyes me with such contempt I would in other circumstances be inclined to sever all contact with her. Yet I need her. She is not my Cleopatra, I know that now, but her face is as near to the original as I am ever likely to get. She is beautiful, especially when she is dressed as my beloved queen. But deep within this woman lies a darkness, a blackness of soul such as I have never before encountered. It disturbs me greatly—and so does she.

Around Adeline, the library was silent except for the crackling of the logs in the fire. She looked at her watch. Eleven-fifteen. Time to put her plan into action. Her stomach churned with butterflies. Deception and duplicity were not in her nature, but she had to do as the professor and she had agreed.

Outside the library, the hall was empty. No sign of Butters or Magda. Before she could lose her nerve, she made her way to the servant's entrance and paused on the short landing. Taking a deep breath, she picked up her skirt and carefully made her way down the flight of stone steps. The warming aroma of roasting meat wafted up and the clatter of pans told her the cook was about.

At her approach, the woman looked up from her pastry-making. "Madam?"

The voice belonged to a much younger woman than Adeline had expected. She had drawn her black hair into a tight bun, and wore a clean, white apron over a long mauve dress. Her sleeves were rolled up to her elbows, exposing olive skin. Her face was unlined, with distinctive dark blue—no, violet—eyes.

"Frau Lederer?" Adeline's mouth ran dry. There was something familiar about this woman.

"Yes? What can I do for you?"

The dark eyes scrutinized her.

Adeline swallowed. "I came down to say that I won't be in for dinner again tomorrow, and also to introduce myself. I have been here for six weeks and we have never met." Adeline completed her descent of the steps, dropped her skirt and put out her hand to the cook, who ignored it. "I am Adeline Ogilvy."

"Yes, madam. I know." The woman spoke with a noticeable accent. German was clearly not her first language, despite her Teutonic surname.

Adeline lowered her hand and glanced around the immaculate kitchen. On the walls, copper pans gleamed. Shelves, laden with all manner of bowls, dishes and plates, spoke of a busy household, not the quiet almost uninhabited one that remained. Indeed, when had it ever required so much kitchen equipment?

Light filtered into the room from two large windows, through which steps leading up to ground level were visible.

At the far end of the kitchen, a fire burned brightly and Magda sat on a chair, quietly mending a pillowcase.

Butters hurried into the room. His expression sour.

"Can we help you, madam?"

"I came to tell Frau Lederer that I would not be in for dinner tomorrow. I forgot to mention it to you this morning, Butters, and I didn't want her to go to any trouble on my account."

"That is quite all right, madam. Isn't it, Frau Lederer?"

The two exchanged glances, impossible for Adeline to read. "Indeed, Herr Butters," the cook replied.

The two stared at her. Magda carried on sewing. She hadn't even acknowledged Adeline's presence.

Adeline's palms tingled. Standing there, she experienced a strange—almost surreal—sensation. If those three had disappeared in a puff of smoke, it wouldn't have seemed any more bizarre than her current feelings. Out of place. Out of time.

"Thank you," she said. The cook and the butler stood, unmoving, while she climbed the stairs. She could feel their eyes burning into her. Needles prickled her skin, but she would not hurry. She closed the door, sweat breaking out on her forehead. Adeline wiped it away with a cursory flick of her hand, then strained to hear any conversation that might start after her departure, but the wood was too solid to make out any sound on the other side of it.

At Café Central the following evening, she reported her experiences to the professor, and then dropped her bombshell. She had been going over it again and again and always came up with the same conclusion.

"I'm almost sure Frau Lederer was the model for the portrait of Cleopatra."

She expected the professor to react in some way. He didn't.

"I am not surprised, because I suspected things were not as they should be there," he said. "My friend has been researching into the genealogy of the butler and the cook. His findings are quite extraordinary and certainly defy easy explanation."

"What were they? What did he find?"

"You must understand first that Professor Martin Lansdowne is the finest, the very finest in his field. If he cannot trace someone's lineage, then, believe me, it doesn't exist."

"What do you mean? They *do* exist. You've met Butters."

"Neither of them has any traceable past. Of course, they may have changed their names. But that begs the question, why? Why would an innocent butler and cook go to considerable trouble to conceal their true identity?"

"They must have something to hide."

"Clearly. But what?"

Adeline shook her head. "I can't imagine, but Dr. Quintillus was, as we know, a ruthless murderer. They have both been with him some years. Maybe they occupied another, more sinister role in his life at some time."

"My belief entirely. This evidence—or more accurately, lack of it—coupled with your experiences yesterday serve to convince me that they know far more than is yet clear to us. The precise nature of their role I could not possibly speculate, yet. But I will caution you to be very careful around them. It is probably best that you keep away from any return visit to the kitchen. I would also like Professor Lansdowne to research the girl. Magda. Do you know her surname?"

"She told me it's Varga, and she has never been married. But she didn't join the household until after the doctor died, so I can't believe she would have any role in this…whatever it is."

"Nevertheless, when we consider the sources of the assertions that she only came to the household recently, we cannot hold them to be accurate. Maybe she did, maybe she didn't. Perhaps she's innocent, perhaps not. We first have to be sure who our enemy is if we are going to defeat him, or her."

That made sense to Adeline. As much as anything did these days. "She's Hungarian. From a small village near Budapest, but I'm afraid I don't know the name of it."

"No matter. I'm sure Professor Lansdowne will work his magic with what little we do know. I shall telephone him tomorrow morning. As soon as I receive a response, we can plan our next course of action. Has anything else happened in the house?"

Adeline shook her head. "It's been quiet. A bit too quiet sometimes. In the library, I quite often feel the atmosphere is so thick I could slice through it."

"I hope you don't stay there after you have dined?"

"No, and I haven't seen that picture again, either. For which I am most relieved."

When Adeline returned, the house was in darkness. She switched on the light in the hall.

Butters came out of the library. He wore his usual dour expression. This time he wasn't alone.

"We have been waiting for you. Please come in."

He stood aside. Adeline hesitated. But where could she run to? There would be no more trams tonight. It was freezing outside and she wouldn't stand a chance out there on her own.

"I was going to bed," she said.

"Please come in here."

Polite coldness. Was it really any icier out in the street?

Adeline turned to the front door and touched the handle. It refused to budge.

Then Butters was at her shoulder. "There is no point. Come with me."

She moved like an automaton. She willed herself to stand still, but his voice paralyzed her somehow. He seemed to take control of her movements so that her legs refused to obey her and drove her inexorably on. She fought against it, but still her feet dragged her closer to the library, where Frau Lederer was waiting for her.

The cook's uniform had been replaced by a long black dress, high-necked and long sleeved. Frau Lederer said nothing but moved gracefully toward the far end of the room.

"What do you want?" Adeline said at last, trying to keep her voice steady, mostly failing.

"Come with us," Butters said, nudging her forward. Yet again her legs obeyed him and her feet stumbled over the rug and then the polished floor.

The basement door opened by itself, swinging wide. Adeline tried to force her brain to obey her, but her unsteady gait took her onward, close behind the cook.

"Who are you?" Adeline asked. She grasped the handrail.

No reply.

At the end of the corridor, the room that had always been in darkness was now lit. Maybe a hundred candles illuminated the walls and hieroglyphics as Adeline had never before seen them. She had seen pictures of some archeological digs in Egypt over the years and clearly this entire room had been modeled on an actual tomb. Maybe Cleopatra's.

The portrait that so haunted her hung on the wall—its face in profile.

Frau Lederer motioned Adeline to a gilt, high-backed chair she didn't remember seeing before. Unable to stop herself, she sat. Terror coated every pore of her body. Sweat broke out on her forehead and palms. She gripped the arms of the chair.

Frau Lederer began to chant. Although Adeline couldn't understand a word, she knew she had heard it before, in the same, strange language.

She tried again. "What do you want from me?"

They did not answer. On the far side of the room a door slowly opened.

A tall figure in a stovepipe hat crossed into the room. His eyeless sockets black and empty. His whole arid presence devoid of humanity. He moved toward her. Something tickled the back of her neck and crawled around to the front. Adeline's arms wouldn't move, but she could turn her head. A black metallic-looking beetle perched on her shoulder.

Chapter 9

Adeline woke with a start. Where was she? Her eyes focused on the walls of her room in Vienna. She pushed the sheet and blanket aside and looked down at her crumpled nightgown with no recollection of getting undressed or going to bed last night. Common sense told her she must have dreamed everything. But it had been so real. The cook and the butler. Quintillus. That chanting. She shook her head, trying to clear it, went over to the window and drew back the drapes on a dry morning with a pale yellow sun promising fine weather.

Her shoulder itched and stung. She'd been bitten by some insect. Mosquitoes in February? Adeline donned her dressing gown and made her way to the bathroom. In the mirror, she saw two little puncture marks, angry red in color and swollen into two small balls of fire forming lumps on her shoulder. When she touched them, pain shot down her arm. She bathed her skin, relishing the soothing caress of the warm water and, as she did so, she remembered the beetle on her shoulder. That, at least, had to be true.

Back in her room, she stripped off the bedding, but found nothing except a couple of blood spots on the sheet. Adeline remade the bed, dressed and put on her shoes. Her arm throbbed. She must find something to relieve it.

She checked the time. Just before eight thirty. Butters would be arriving with her breakfast in the library, but he was the last person she wanted to mention this to.

As she left her room, she caught sight of something near the fireplace. She went over and bent down. A sizeable beetle, its carapace shiny black with iridescent green flecks. A scarab—maybe the same one that bit her last night. She must show it to Professor Mayer. Adeline looked around for something to put it in and found it. A matchbox. Using a handkerchief, she carefully picked up the dead insect and placed it in the box, which she returned to the mantelpiece.

Her arm throbbed more violently. Down in the hall, she caught a glimpse of Butters as he disappeared back to the kitchen. Magda was polishing the table. She would have to do.

"Magda, I've been bitten by a beetle. Is there anything in the house I can put on it to make it less painful?"

"I'll ask Frau Lederer," the maid replied.

Adeline couldn't allow that. "No, no, don't trouble her. She's much too busy. Is there nothing in the house to treat bites?"

Magda thought for a moment. "I think I know of something. I'll go and get it."

"Thank you." Adeline hoped and prayed Magda was precisely who she claimed to be and that whatever she brought wouldn't do any more damage than had already been inflicted.

———

Wincing at the stinging, burning pain in her arm, Adeline went into the library and recoiled. The smell of lilies stifled the heavy atmosphere. Butters and Frau Lederer stood at the far side of the room in front of the window.

Frau Lederer was dressed in the long black gown she had worn last night. "Come to us," she said, her voice more heavily accented than before.

Adeline shook her head.

"You will come to us." Butters' tone was firm and commanding. Adeline's brain swam with its hypnotic effect. She had to go to them.

The strange surrealism returned. Her head seemed suspended in some sort of cloud, trapped in a body that would no longer obey her.

They led her down to the basement and into the room where the hieroglyphics adorned the walls and the portrait—now removed from the wall—was propped up on an altar of deep purple velvet. Once again, a forest of candles lit up every corner. A small whimper Adeline recognized as hers, punctured the heavy atmosphere. She could make no protest, no other cry, even though her mind screamed at her to get out.

A tug on her arm and the sound of tearing cotton. Frau Lederer had ripped off the sleeve of her dress. The insect bite throbbed and burned. Metal gleamed, and Butters raised a sharp dagger.

Adeline braced herself. She refused to show fear to this man. To do so would give him even more power over her than he already possessed. She closed her eyes. In a few seconds, an instant's sharp pain, and warm blood and pus trickled down to her wrist. She opened her eyes in time to watch it splash into a small golden bowl, held by the cook. The incision had released the pressure building up in her infected arm and Adeline almost swooned with the relief it brought. The flow of blood slowed to a mere trickle and then stopped. Frau Lederer silently removed the bowl and placed it on the altar.

She dipped her right forefinger into it and touched the portrait so that a red smear appeared on the cheek of the subject. Neither the cook nor the butler had uttered a word since they had brought her down here. Both began to chant as before. Butters steered Adeline to the gilt chair she had dreamed she had sat in the previous day. *If* she had indeed dreamed it.

A shape began to form in one corner of the room.

Frau Lederer clutched a small gold statue to her chest and her body began to heave. Adeline's eyes stung. The room filled with the familiar eerie green radiance. It pulsed with new urgency. The figure formed itself into the jackal head atop the body of a man. Set waited silently in front of her. Expressionless. Statuesque. Real.

Adeline's vision clouded. She wanted to rub her eyes, but her hands wouldn't move from her lap.

The cook moved in front of her, still chanting. Butters joined her. Adeline's vision blurred. Pyramids, desert, and shadows of people who belonged as decoration on an ancient tomb's walls floated impossibly before her eyes, their form shadowy and at times indistinct as if transmitted from faraway. The chanting died away and the images faded with it. Adeline was left in the basement that had become her prison. Set stood—a silent, forbidding sentinel cloaked in a green, pulsating glow.

Butters spoke to Frau Lederer in their strange, archaic language. The cook handed over the portrait of the queen to him. Behind him, the figure of Set faded. No more pulsing light. The atmosphere lifted and Adeline's fingers flexed.

Butters held the portrait above his head, then without warning, brought it down and smashed it on the altar.

Adeline and the cook cried out. Frau Lederer brandished the statue.

Butters drew back his fist and smashed it into the cook's face. She fell heavily and the statue dropped from her hands and clattered to the floor. Released from her paralysis, Adeline jumped up, balled her fist and landed a punch on the butler's chin. She tried to run but her foot snagged in the hem of her skirt and he caught her before she could escape.

"You stupid woman, I'm trying to save your life."

He twisted her arms tightly behind her back. Adeline struggled but his grip was too firm. Her anger had reached boiling point. If she could kick him, knee him in the groin or hit him again she would, but he held her too firmly.

"Let me go. Let me out of here!"

From the floor where she lay, semi-conscious, the cook moaned.

"You could have killed her," Adeline said, still struggling to free herself.

"Would to heaven I had," Butters said. "Believe me, it would be better for you if she never left this room."

That was unexpected. "But you're both involved in this…this…whatever it is. This attempt to bring Cleopatra back to life."

"You really don't understand anything, do you?" Butters manhandled Adeline. She fought his grip on her.

"Let go of me!" Adeline staggered as the butler unexpectedly released his hold.

The cook cried out. The bloodstained dagger glinted in her hand.

Butters staggered backward and gripped the gilt chair.

Nothing stood between the wild-eyed woman and Adeline. The cook gripped the weapon tighter.

Adeline backed away. Her voice rang out around the room, thankfully firm and strong. "Who are you?"

The door flew open and a shot rang out. The woman dropped the dagger. For a few seconds, Adeline's eyes met with hers. She read a mix of fear and incomprehension before the cook fell dead at her feet.

Adeline stared at the sprawled figure on the floor. In the chair, the butler stirred. A rustling of skirts and Magda dashed past, dropping her small pistol in the process. She cradled Butters' head. "Can you hear me, Mr. Butters?"

The butler gave a faint nod.

Adeline stared at the maid as if she had never seen her before. Gone was the frightened mouse of a girl. Magda took charge. She eased off the butler's jacket to the slightest of protests from the semi-conscious man "It seems to be a flesh wound," she said, peering at the blood-drenched gash in the butler's back, an inch or two below his right shoulder. "Not too deep, thankfully. He must have twisted away at the right moment. Nevertheless I think we should try and get him upstairs. Into the library at least. Can you help me?"

Adeline nodded. Questions demanded to be answered, but not now.

Between them, they half-carried the butler. Back in the library, they set him down on a leather settee.

"I will telephone for the doctor," Magda said.

"But, what about Frau Lederer? We can't leave her there."

"No. I will deal with her. Later. We have more urgent business with the living than the dead in this house."

Magda left Adeline alone with Butters. He stirred and opened his eyes.

"Mrs. Ogilvy."

"Yes, Butters. I'm here. Magda is telephoning for the doctor. Frau Lederer stabbed you with the dagger you used on me."

Adeline looked down at her bloodstained arm. Astounded, she couldn't locate the actual wound. Just a trickle of dried blood.

"Scarab," the butler said. "*She* brought it to you."

"Frau Lederer?"

"Not Frau Lederer. Arsinoe."

"I don't understand. Who is Arsinoe?"

The butler closed his eyes and slipped back into unconsciousness.

A few minutes later, he was still out when the doctor arrived. He examined Butters, requested hot water and clean towels and, while Adeline sat quietly on the Chesterfield, he worked on the butler. Magda stood nearby.

The doctor looked up, a frown creasing his face. "You say your cook did this?"

"Yes, Doctor," Magda replied.

"And where is she now? Do the police have her?"

"She ran away," Magda said before Adeline could respond. Out of sight of the doctor, the maid shook her head at Adeline, who said nothing.

"Then I must report this incident to the police so that they can apprehend this woman."

"Yes, Doctor," Magda lowered her eyes.

His wound bandaged and consciousness beginning once again to return, the doctor and Magda helped Butters to his room, where he was under orders to stay in bed for the next few days.

When the doctor left, Magda joined Adeline in the library.

Adeline motioned her to sit down. "Will you please tell me what's going on?"

The maid took a deep breath and began, "Since I came to this place, I have seen things I can barely believe. The dead walk in this house."

"You've seen Dr. Quintillus?"

The girl shuddered. "I think so. When I first came here, I decided to go exploring and I wish to God I hadn't." She crossed herself.

"Butters and Frau Lederer. Who are they really?"

"Mr. Butters is a strange one. He seems so stern, but I believe he can be kind. He was attracted to Frau Lederer for a long time. He believed they had met in a previous life—in ancient Egypt. He told me he had found a way of returning them to their original selves, so that they could be together as they never could in this world. But that's when it all went wrong. He found out Frau Lederer was not who she claimed to be. Oh, I expect she had been Josefa Lederer at one time. She was certainly *somebody*, but Butters became convinced that the person who inhabited her body was not the person she was born as."

"He mentioned something—or someone—called Arsinoe."

Magda's eyes flashed. "Yes. That's the name. Arsinoe."

"Who is she? Do you know?"

"No, madam. I don't, but Mr. Butters told me yesterday that he was becoming most concerned about Frau Lederer. He mentioned that name and said he believed she had designs on killing you."

"But why? I've done nothing to the woman."

"I said the dead walk this house. You've seen so yourself, haven't you? Mr. Butters is charged with carrying out his late master's instructions and Frau Lederer—or whoever was using her body— seems to have been determined to stop him. He played along with her. He didn't want to arouse her suspicions, but when she sent that scarab to bite you, he knew he had to act. He also took the precaution of telling me their plans for today. If anything went wrong, he told me I must kill her. He said he would smash the picture and that would be my cue. I was waiting outside the door, listening. Mr. Butters told me he thought Frau Lederer planned to do away with you, using a death spell. For Dr. Quintillus's plan to work, the ritual should have gone differently. You should have been transformed by the blood and dust into a host body for the spirit of the queen Cleopatra, but Mr. Butters was right. Frau Lederer—or Arsinoe—had other plans."

Adeline remembered the dead woman in the basement. "What are we going to do about her? Let the police find her?"

"And go to prison for the rest of my life? I would rather not, madam, if you don't mind. Leave her to me. I will dispose of her. My two brothers will help me."

A dark thought flashed through Adeline's brain. "Can we really be sure she's dead?"

Magda stared at her and in that brief exchange, Adeline knew they shared the same fears. Whoever—or whatever—Arsinoe was, she had the power to possess the mind and body of another, and if she could do that, how could she be lying dead in that basement?

The awful realization of the impact of Magda's actions, seemed to hit them both at the same moment. Surely they would soon feel the full force of the wrath of the ancient ones—a force that had reduced Quintillus to some kind of living corpse and would now be turned against them.

Chapter 10

Professor Mayer struggled to his feet as Adeline approached his table in Café Central. Nearby, she caught a familiar face. Dr. Trotsky inclined his head and smiled. His companion—Dr. Adler—moved a black knight on the chessboard and clapped his hands in triumph. Dr. Trotsky raised his eyes to heaven.

"Yet again, you have me at a disadvantage, Herr Doktor," he said, winking at Adeline.

Adeline shook the professor's hand and sat.

"You are acquainted with Leon Trotsky?" the professor asked.

"Not really. He picked up a glove I dropped on my first visit here. Seems a good sort."

"I'm not sure I would describe him in quite that way myself," the professor said, "although he is certainly possessed of a formidable intellect. I have a strong feeling the world will hear much more of him before the century is too much older. Anyway, my dear, we have not come to talk of that. I know you have news you couldn't reveal to me over the telephone. Tell me what happened."

Adeline glanced around. As always, the café was busy. The noise of clinking china, chatter and laughter would effectively drown out their conversation. Coffee and cakes arrived, the waiter moved away and the professor let his espresso grow cold as he listened in rapt attention to Adeline's account of all that had happened to her and Magda. She left nothing out. At the end of it, Professor Mayer took a gulp of his cold coffee and wiped his mouth on his napkin.

"So where is the… Where is Frau Lederer now?"

"As far as I know—and hope—still in the basement. Magda's two brothers are coming tomorrow. They're traveling from Hungary."

"And the statue?"

Adeline lowered her eyes. "I'm sorry, Professor, I was so concerned to get out of there, I forgot it. It's probably still down there."

"We can attend to that later, my dear. What did the police do?"

"I have never come across such sloppy police work in my life. Naturally, we didn't tell them that Butters was stabbed in the basement. Magda told them that Frau Lederer and Butters had a row in the kitchen and that the cook had a sharp kitchen knife in her hand at the time. She stabbed Butters and then, realizing what she'd done, made her getaway. Magda gave them a fairly bland description of what she looked like and they went away."

"Didn't they think it odd that there was no blood and no knife?"

"Magda apologized that she had cleaned up because she didn't want to leave the kitchen dirty. I must say she is a much better actress than I would have given her credit for. She played dumb so well I almost believed her."

"I'm afraid that where the victim is a servant and the assailant is too, very little interest is taken. Did they interview the butler?"

"Magda said the doctor had given strict instructions he wasn't to be roused for at least another seventy-two hours. She said he had put him under sedation."

"And they didn't question that? Or ask to see him?"

"No. As I said, very sloppy. They said they would be back in three or four days. Personally, I doubt it."

"How is Butters after his ordeal?"

"He drifts in and out of consciousness. I'm sure his injury isn't severe enough for this reaction and I'm convinced there is something more at work here. Butters has angered the dark forces, and now he must pay their price."

The professor nodded. "Let's go back to something you said earlier. Butters mentioned the name 'Arsinoe'?"

"Yes. Is it familiar to you?"

"Most definitely. You see, Arsinoe was one of Cleopatra's sisters. The two were bitter rivals and hated each other. Arsinoe even managed to have herself proclaimed queen of Egypt at one point, so Cleopatra had her killed."

"And Butters must believe that Frau Lederer is Arsinoe returned to life."

"It would appear so."

"Professor, I can't stay in that house anymore. Butters may not want me dead, but he obviously wants to carry out Dr. Quintillus's instructions—if he even survives. Frau Lederer should, by all reason, be dead, but something tells me that is not the end of the story. I know Magda feels the same. These curses are all too real. Then there's the statue…"

"Would it help if I stayed in the house with you?"

Adeline could have kissed him. "Oh yes, indeed, Professor. Butters is hardly in a position to protest, and I'm quite sure Magda won't be put out. I think she might even welcome your presence and knowledge, maybe as much as I will."

"Then it shall be done. I shall move in tomorrow."

Adeline resisted a strong urge to kiss the elderly man. "Thank you. I don't know how I shall ever repay your kindness."

"Not at all, my dear. This is a most fascinating experience and at some time in the near future, I shall commission you to type it all up for me. I'm quite sure we will have publishers queuing up."

Adeline managed a smile. She felt a little easier now that Professor Mayer would be there to help navigate them all through whatever lay ahead.

Magda was waiting for her when she arrived home. Adeline could tell from the trembling lips and frown that something significant had happened while she was out.

"The doctor has just left. Mr. Butters suffered a heart attack and died an hour ago."

Adeline clamped her hand over her mouth, then released it. She had been right, and now Butters had paid the ultimate price. "How did it happen?"

"I went up with some soup and he seemed to be sleeping peacefully, but something in the room felt wrong. There was this strong smell of lilies, which, as you know, Mr. Butters associates with death, and something wrong with the way the moonlight shone into the room."

"Moonlight? It's cloudy tonight; there isn't any."

"That's what I mean. But there was this greenish glow."

The hairs on the back of Adeline's neck prickled. "Tell me the rest of it."

Magda swallowed. "I can't explain why or what caused it, but Mr. Butters sat bolt upright, as if someone had dragged him up by his shoulders. He opened his eyes, stared straight ahead and screamed. Oh, madam, it was an awful sound. I could swear he saw some awful creature, but there was nothing else in the room except me, and he wasn't looking in my direction. Then, he took one mighty breath, clutched his chest and sort of…crumpled. He didn't fall back. It was like someone had laid him down. His eyes closed. I could swear some hand shut them, and then his mouth closed. But I knew he was dead, even before that light faded."

On impulse, Adeline put her arms around the maid, who sobbed quietly into her shoulder. Adeline offered up a silent prayer and struggled to quash the rising tide of panic surging up from her stomach.

Adeline didn't see Butters' body. A firm of undertakers collected it later that evening. The following morning, Professor Mayer arrived at around eleven. He seemed unsurprised at what had happened to the butler. "Of course, we still don't know exactly who he really was," he said to Adeline and Magda.

Magda smoothed her apron. "I know who he *said* he was," she said.

Adeline and the professor's eyes turned to her.

Magda shrugged. "For what it's worth, he told me he was a convicted criminal. His name was James Wadsworth and he was convicted of stealing jewelry in London in 1905. He escaped from prison and Dr. Quintillus took him in. Apparently, the two of them had met some years earlier in Oxford. Mr. Butters had valeted for him, or so he told me. Dr. Quintillus told him he was moving to Vienna and he could go with him, change his identity and so on. Mr. Butters told me how grateful he had been for that second chance."

The professor tapped his stick. "In return, the late doctor gets a faithful servant who will do anything he requests of him. When did he tell you all this, Magda?"

"Just before everything happened in the basement. At the same time he told me about Frau Lederer and made me promise I would shoot her if she tried to kill Mrs. Ogilvy."

"You are handy with a pistol then, Magda?"

The maid smiled. "I grew up on a small farm. I used to shoot rats as a child."

The doorbell rang and Magda went to answer it, returning a short time later accompanied by two burly men in dusty clothes, carrying a rolled-up carpet.

"My brothers, Istvan and Ferenc. This is Mrs. Ogilvy and Professor Mayer."

Adeline and the professor acknowledged them.

The two men exchanged words in Hungarian with their sister. Three oil lamps stood in readiness on the desk, and each of them took one.

The professor nudged Adeline. "I think we should go with them, my dear. It may be necessary. And we can retrieve the statue at the same time."

Magda spoke. "I know where it is. I found it when I went down earlier to check she was still there. I put it in a safe place."

"Now we know where it is, don't you think we should equip ourselves with the statue first before attempting to move her?" Adeline asked. "If it really is as powerful as you believe, we may need its protection."

"Good point, my dear," Professor Mayer said.

Adeline helped the professor to his feet and Magda and her brothers waited, lit lamps in their hands, until all five of them could proceed down together.

The basement room gave off a new foul odor this time. Frau Lederer still lay where she had fallen. Magda ignored her and moved swiftly over to the far wall where she bent down. She scrabbled under some broken boxes and pulled something out. The lamplight reflected the gleam of gold.

Magda dashed back to where the professor and Adeline stood, side by side.

She thrust it at Professor Mayer. "Here, take it, please. I never want to see it again. The mere feel of it scares me."

He took the statuette from her and turned it over in his hand. "This is a very powerful weapon in the wrong hands, or if used incorrectly."

Magda's brothers bent over the corpse of Frau Lederer. As they moved her to lift her, the stench of evacuated bowels set Adeline and Magda retching.

The professor seemed unfazed. "Ah, that is nothing compared to the smell of a freshly exposed mummy."

The men unrolled their carpet and lifted the body onto it. They made to roll it up when it suddenly moved. The men jumped back, crossing themselves. Magda screamed. The corpse's white face gleamed in the light. It sat up, turned its head and opened its mouth. A single shiny, scarab crawled out, then another and another, until scarabs were crawling all over the corpse. Adeline backed away. The others looked on, horrified. Only the professor seemed fascinated. Without a word, he pointed the statue at the corpse and muttered some words Adeline didn't understand. The scarabs vanished. The corpse went limp and exhaled a rush of ordure-drenched air. It lay back, much as Adeline imagined Butters' body must have lain back that final time.

"You can remove her," the professor said, "She shouldn't cause you any more harm."

Magda translated for her brothers. The men hesitated, but Magda reassured them. They nodded over to the professor who nodded back.

"Look, Professor!" Adeline pointed to the far corner of the room behind the two men. The all-too familiar aura was forming, and a black shadow grew beside it. Shapeless. Filling half the wall in a couple of seconds.

"I see it," the professor said. "Magda, your brothers need to work quickly. We must leave this place."

The two men lifted the carpet-wrapped body to shoulder height and hurried as best they could with their heavy burden. Magda grabbed two of the lamps and Adeline retrieved the third.

She caught a glimpse of the smashed portrait on the makeshift altar. The splintered frame crackled as shards of wood knitted together to reform. The female profile held captive within flashed into full face… glaring from the canvas. Adeline cried out a warning as the shadow crept down the wall and slicked across the floor toward them.

"Professor!"

Professor Mayer held the statue up high. He retreated as fast as his limp would allow. He repeated the spell. A low, guttural laugh grated on Adeline's ears.

An unfamiliar male voice echoed after them down the corridor. "You can do nothing to me. *Nothing*. She is already mine."

Adeline slammed the door behind them and locked it.

Magda hurried her brothers through the library and out into the dark, silent street. Light snow fell as the men loaded their grisly burden onto their horse-drawn cart. They kissed their sister and climbed into the driving seat, tying scarves tightly around their necks against the cold. Their patient horse obeyed their command and trotted away.

"I wonder where they'll take her," Adeline said.

"A few miles downstream along the Danube," Magda said, as she rejoined Adeline and the professor at the entrance. "Bodies are always turning up. By the time this one does, the fishes will have done their work."

"The woman doesn't even have a confirmed identity," Professor Mayer said.

Magda raised an eyebrow.

"I mean," said the professor, "Professor Lansdowne finally managed to trace a Josefa Lederer listed on a marriage certificate dated 1907. Her husband's name was Anton and their honeymoon was tragically cut short on their wedding night when someone stabbed and killed the young man in an apparently unprovoked attack on a street in the Margareten district here in Vienna. As far as Professor

Lansdowne is aware, the police never apprehended anyone in connection with the attack. His widow then disappeared from public record."

Magda coughed. "Mr. Butters told me Frau Lederer came to work here in late 1907."

Adeline and the professor exchanged glances.

"That would seem to indicate her identity then," the professor said. "One less mystery to solve."

"Could Dr. Quintillus have had anything to do with her husband's death?" Adeline asked.

The professor tapped his stick for a few moments. "Possibly, but I think it unlikely. The timing seems wrong somehow. I no longer believe that Frau Lederer was the model for the Cleopatra portrait. We may never know who that was. You told me he said the woman who would pose for Cleopatra had already been known to him. Right under his nose, so to speak. I doubt the doctor would have been aware of her prior to her coming to work for him and she hadn't been with him very long. I can't see a man like him associating himself too much with the woman who cooked his food. Besides, we now know that the ancient spirit that inhabits Frau Lederer's body is—or rather was—Arsinoe. Who the model was, or where she came from will have to remain a mystery."

"Herr Lederer's death was just a tragic accident then," Adeline said.

"Probably. Maybe her grief left his widow vulnerable to possession in some way. I am no expert in these matters. Now, may we please return to the fire? My hands are turning blue."

The three made their way back into the warmth of the library. Adeline spoke first. "So that's the end of Arsinoe." Even as she said it, she didn't believe it.

Professor Mayer sat and stared into the flames for a moment. "I'm not sure, Adeline. I can only hope so."

"But surely now she really *is* dead. After those beetles..." Adeline shuddered. "We saw her loaded onto the cart."

"Yes, we did, didn't we?"

"Was it all about revenge?" Magda asked. "Arsinoe avenging herself against Cleopatra?"

Both women looked at the professor. Adeline was surprised at the intense way he was staring at Magda. There didn't seem any reason for it. Unless she was imagining it. She dismissed her fears. Too much had transpired these past weeks. She would be screaming at her own shadow next. With a shudder she remembered the latest incident. Would to heaven whatever was still down in that basement left them alone, for at least as long as they needed to get out of that house.

Professor Mayer spoke. "I think you have summed it up fairly accurately, Magda. Arsinoe wanted to see her sister's spirit damned for all time to be tied to the dried-up husk that is Emeryk Quintillus. Butters wanted what his master sought; the curse undone, Quintillus restored to life and Cleopatra's spirit reborn in you, Adeline. Both needed the same ingredients to ensure their plans were fulfilled. As long as the statue stayed with Cleopatra in her tomb, Arsinoe was powerless, but Quintillus's action in removing it freed her sister to attach her spirit to a receptive host. Once here, she found precisely that."

"Frau Lederer," Adeline said.

"Precisely. Which is, of course, why it took Butters so long to realize what was happening. He saw the cook as a devout and loyal servant, and someone to whom he had become increasingly attracted. For her part, Arsinoe lay low for a long while, biding her time. She played her part well. Most convincingly. It must have been a cruel shock for the butler when he realized what had happened to his beloved Josefa. When he heard her chant the death spell, he smashed the portrait, not just to summon Magda but also he thought that, without it, no more harm could be done. Even though it meant his master would not have what he so desperately desired."

"That's why Butters told me he was trying to save my life."

"I believe so, yes. The scroll has been most helpful in illuminating the many facets of the power of that little statue. Without it, I don't think I could have drawn so many conclusions. Although..." The professor's forehead creased.

"What is it?" Adeline asked. "Is there more?"

"I'm not sure. I can't help feeling I've missed something." He shook his head.

Adeline sighed. "At least I can telephone Miss Sinclair and get back to England. I can't see there will be any more work for me here. After all, as you said, Professor, my assignment was only a ruse to get me here."

"I am quite sure you're right," he said. "But we cannot return to England quite yet. We have an important task to perform."

Adeline's rising spirits once more sank. "What task, Professor?"

"We must return the statue to Cleopatra. We must travel to Taposiris Magna without delay."

Chapter 11

Much to her relief, when Adeline telephoned the agency to explain that both the butler and the cook had died, Miss Sinclair expressed sympathy and promised to negotiate with the lawyers. Meanwhile, of course Adeline should have a short break, to recover from her ordeal. As she replaced the receiver, Adeline smiled. Whatever would the down-to-earth woman have made of everything she *hadn't* told her?

Her bags packed, Adeline settled down in bed for her last night in Vienna. The house had been quiet since Butters and Frau Lederer died, but for Adeline daylight couldn't come soon enough. At a little after eight, as Adeline and the professor were eating breakfast in the library, the bell suddenly began ringing repeatedly while someone hammered on the door.

Adeline jumped up, setting the cutlery rattling.

The door burst open and a white-faced Magda dashed in, accompanied by her equally white-faced brothers.

"She has gone!"

The professor struggled to his feet and reached for his stick.

"What do you mean?" Adeline asked. "Who's gone?"

"Frau Lederer. My brothers decided to take her far from here. They rode for nearly a day, never once leaving their cart unattended. Then, when it grew dark again, they went to fetch her body, but she wasn't there. Only the rolled-up carpet remained."

The professor spoke. "Could she have fallen out? When the cart hit a pothole or some other obstacle."

"No, the cart has four sides, all of which are too high for anything to roll out."

Adeline sat down heavily. All her fears flowed back. "Then where is she?"

The professor laid a comforting hand on her arm. "I don't know, my dear, but I suggest we leave. Without delay."

"Yes. Magda, what will you do?"

The maid shook her head. "The only thing I can do is return to Hungary with my brothers. There is nothing for me here anymore. I cannot remain in this house, and I cannot stay in Vienna without a job."

"I think that's a wise decision. Miss Sinclair is contacting the lawyers in London so, if you could secure everything here. I'm sure your brothers will stay with you until you are ready to leave."

"Yes, madam."

A chill wafted through the room and the ghostly words washed back into Adeline's mind.

"*You can do nothing to me.* Nothing. *She is already mine.*"

Quintillus. It must have been him, and he was still down there, somewhere—or what remained of him—wandering through the bowels of the basement. Now the body of Frau Lederer had disappeared, Adeline couldn't help wondering if he had company. Or maybe she would prove to be his nemesis.

As for the portrait... Adeline shivered. Last time she had seen it, those eyes had stared straight through her. Had that picture repaired itself fully? Was it back on the wall? And, most disturbing of all, did Quintillus still intend to recreate his beloved queen?

The professor patted her hand. "Come, my dear. It's time to go. Let's get that statue back where it belongs and end this once and for all. Then the dead can once more rest in peace and we who are living can get on with the rest of our lives."

"Do you truly believe it will all be put right when the statue is returned to Egypt?"

"I have to believe the scroll."

"And it told you this is what will happen."

Did she imagine it, or did the professor hesitate for a second before replying?

"Yes, my dear. It did."

Adeline hated leaving Magda looking so apprehensive. Her future was so uncertain and, with increasing unrest in her country, her prospects were nowhere near as secure as Adeline's.

"Come, my dear, the train won't wait for us." The professor urged Adeline toward the waiting carriage and she and the maid embraced one last time.

Magda and her brothers waved them off until they were out of sight.

In the darkness, at the side of the house, a shadow moved.

Adeline leaned back in the carriage as it took them to the train, which would take them to the port of Trieste and, from there, by ship to Alexandria.

"Where is the statue now, Professor?"

Professor Mayer was frowning. He seemed lost in thought until her question roused him. "I have it in my pocket. I thought it best not to let it out of sight, or at least to retain about my person at all times."

Adeline could imagine little worse than having that thing so close to her. At this moment, though, the professor's expression bothered her.

"What is it, Professor?

He sighed. "Oh, probably nothing, my dear. I shall be relieved when we have performed our task and can put this all behind us."

"I don't see how we can return it to the queen, though. We don't know where her tomb lies and, even if we did, it's covered by tons of rubble. Dr. Quintillus's memoirs said so."

"I think we must trust in the powers of the ancients. I believe when we get there, we will be guided. The power that exists there is so great, it will not let us fail."

"But what if the power that does not want this to happen is also there. What if Arsinoe manages to somehow manifest herself?"

"Then we shall have to take appropriate measures to prevent her from interfering with our purpose."

"Something about this is still worrying you, Professor. Won't you tell me what it is?"

He gazed at her steadily. He seemed to be weighing up what he should say and what he should keep to himself. He made his decision.

"Very well, I thought we would encounter much greater resistance. I felt sure Quintillus would try and stop us. Merely shouting after us didn't seem an adequate response to what he would see as the theft of the statue."

"Unless he no longer needed it. Maybe it had served its purpose."

"Perhaps. Yes, you may indeed be right."

"That house is still a dangerous place to be—and will continue to be so, even if we are successful in returning the statue to Cleopatra's tomb. As far as I can tell, all that will do is stop her spirit from wandering aimlessly and reunite her with her body. Quintillus will remain an evil presence within the walls of that house."

The professor sighed. "Yes, sadly that is true. Although thankfully you will not be there and, without a direct descendant of Cleopatra, or the statue, he will be unable to enact his wish."

"The portrait is still there. I told you, it was in full face when I last saw it and repairing itself impossible as that might seem. It still holds considerable power."

"Yes, I will confess, that painting bothers me more and more. Clearly it did not exist when the scroll was written, but the writer does emphasize the power of the dust." The professor stared out of the carriage window as they sped past the rain-soaked countryside. "So now we leave Vienna. Judging by the unrest and disquieting rumors circulating this city, I am guessing many more will be leaving soon—albeit for very different reasons than ours."

"Rumors?"

"You have been too wrapped up in events closer to home, but the threat of war moves ever closer. The Serbians are becoming bolder in their demands for independence. Given the alliances between the various European nations, I cannot help but agree with those who believe the largest war we have ever known in our lifetimes—possibly in the history of the world as we know it — is about to be unleashed and I am very much afraid that, if the revolutionaries in this country and Russia have their way, there may be far fewer monarchs at the end of it."

"Surely not our own King!" Unthinkable.

The professor leaned over and patted her hand. "It is to be hoped that the British throne is secure enough, at least for now, but Russia is quite another matter, as indeed is Austria-Hungary. The Tsar of Russia makes catastrophic errors of judgment, and the old Emperor cannot live forever. His successor — Archduke Franz Ferdinand — is hardly the most popular heir to the throne. I cannot see either of them surviving a war. Still, there is nothing we can do about it. Events will unfold as they will." He sighed and leaned back in his seat again.

"One thing is for sure," Adeline said, "I shall never be able to return there. To that house."

"No, my dear, under no circumstances must you ever return, or to Vienna. Not *ever*."

The vehemence with which he spoke those words disturbed Adeline. Not that she had any intention of returning, but to be told so forcefully that she *must* not, concerned her more than she was prepared to admit.

The professor looked as if he might be about to say more. Adeline steeled herself. Whatever was troubling him, she had to find out.

"What is it, Professor?"

He patted her hand. "Very well. I suppose it is only right you hear it all. Even though it will probably damage your high opinion of me. You see, I am as fallible and capable of making a mistake — and a grave one at that — as anyone else. When I read the hieroglyphics in that room, I believed they related to Cleopatra. That they were her words. But…"

"But if not hers, whose were they?"

The professor shook his head. "That is a question for which I have no answer. I looked for it on the scroll, but I found that it is torn at the bottom. It seems to end, but I believe a piece may be missing. One that could answer that very question, and who knows what else I might have unraveled? I only hope it isn't significant enough to change the task we are undertaking."

"Including, perhaps, how to get rid of Dr. Quintillus once and for all."

"Indeed, my dear. All we can do is hope he remains trapped down there."

The carriage arrived at the station, which seethed with passengers. The professor and Adeline found a porter for their luggage and followed him to their train. Professor Mayer had purchased first class tickets for them, and they quickly found their compartment, where they settled back and prepared for their journey. The professor set his briefcase up on the luggage rack. "I must keep the scroll with me at all times," he said. Then he patted his jacket pocket. "And the statue is safely tucked away here."

Apprehension filled Adeline, especially with the professor's so recently revealed fears. Normally, she, who had never traveled anywhere out of England until she came to Vienna, would have felt excited at the prospect of visiting somewhere new. Instead, she couldn't wait to see the familiar grays and blacks of smoky London.

Chapter 12

Magda trudged back into the house. Istvan and Ferenc stayed outside to attend to their horse and their sister closed the door, without locking it.

She returned to the library, yawning. Soon she would pack her suitcase and leave this place forever. But for now... exhaustion overwhelmed her, and she sank down onto the Chesterfield. The fire crackled and the flames warmed her. She leaned back and her eyes refused to stay open. Maybe a few minutes rest would give her the energy she needed to pack her few belongings and lock up the house. Its contents could stay there. Let the doctor's lawyers deal with all of that. Magda had been through enough for the employer she had never met.

She awoke with a start. The fire had died down to faintly glowing embers. She must have been asleep for an hour or more and one look at the clock told her she was right. Nearly two hours had elapsed. Surely Istvan and Ferenc must be in by now. Magda looked around her and rubbed her eyes. She stood up, stretching limbs that had stiffened. Suddenly she became aware of something behind her. She turned and cried out.

An emerald incandescence illuminated the wall. It pulsated like a heartbeat. Silhouetted against it, in profile, stood a shadow of a man with an animal's head, dressed like an ancient Egyptian. In an instant, she knew this must be the god Set the professor had spoken of.

Magda screamed. "What do you want from me?"

The shadow remained unmoving. The glow continued to pulsate. Someone hammered at the door. The handle rattled.

Ferenc's frantic voice. "*Magda.* Open the door."

"I can't," she replied. "There's...something...blocking my way."

"Magda! You have to try. It won't open."

A sudden draft of cold air hit her from behind. Instinctively, she turned to the source.

The door by the window stood wide open. A dim light shone through. Then the entrance wasn't empty anymore. A tall figure stood there. Familiar in her long black dress.

"Frau Lederer! But how?"

The woman smiled and held out her hand. "Come, my child, you'll be safe with me."

Every instinct and pore of her being told her to ignore the woman's words, but the pulsating green grew stronger. The shadow began to turn toward her. It took on form. Any second and it would be as real as Magda herself.

Magda screamed again. A mighty crash. Istvan and Ferenc were battering the door down. It bowed and creaked but did not give. Whatever controlled this had made sure she would be trapped inside.

Except she wasn't. Not completely.

"Come, my child. I will keep you safe," the cook said.

Magda looked frantically back and forth between the rapidly coalescing figure of Set and the friendly smile of Frau Lederer.

Set took a step away from the wall.

Magda grabbed her skirt and ran to the former cook.

The woman grasped her hand and propelled her through the door. It slammed shut behind them.

"Where are you taking me?"

Frau Lederer didn't answer. She dragged Magda down the stairs and along the corridor. Her grip was not the friendly clasp of someone who wanted to protect her.

The cook shoved Magda into the room at the end of the corridor. She tripped and sprawled across the floor. Tears sprang to her eyes.

The former cook's eyes filled with contempt. "You didn't really think I came to save you, did you? That I would forgive what you did to me? Here. In this basement."

"But that wasn't you. You were possessed. That woman…"

"Arsinoe?"

Magda nodded. "She took you over. You're not a bad person. I know that."

The woman tossed back her head and laughed. Raucous. Harsh. Magda cringed.

"You killed this body."

"But you weren't dead. My brothers…"

"Your brothers are fools. They know nothing of my power. Or the power of the great god, Set. This body was dead. This body remains dead." Frau Lederer bent down and grabbed Magda's hand. She placed it over her heart.

"Try and find it all you may, but you will feel no heartbeat. No fresh air fills my lungs."

The ice cold of the woman's hand almost froze Magda's fingers. The cook's chest was still. No heartbeat. No rise and fall to show she was breathing. Magda stared at her in horror.

The woman released her hand.

"You killed me and now it is your turn."

The room filled with the sickly light. A dark, shadowy cloud formed at the entrance to the room. It writhed and twisted until it settled into the figure of Set. The god moved forward. The ground quaked when he moved. His eyes flashed red fire and Magda silently prayed.

The woman stepped aside. Set raised his arm. A blistering white flame shot from the end of his staff. Magda screamed. Flames erupted all around her, trapping her in their midst. They licked at the fabric of her dress. It caught alight and they spread upward…hungry to consume her body. The woman watched and laughed as Magda's mind seared with agonizing shards of pain.

She struggled to speak. "Hail Mary, full of grace…" No more words would come.

Her mouth filled with bubbling, hot blood. She writhed and twisted, trying to escape, but the unearthly fire held her firm in its grasp. Through dimming eyes, she saw her blistered and burned skin sizzle and shrink from her bones. Her cries became pitiful wails as what remained of her sanity mercifully deserted her.

Smoke filled her nostrils and burned her already ruined throat. Magda's scorched lungs collapsed as blackness descended and her soul begged for release.

Chapter 13

Adeline woke with a start. The rhythmic clattering of the train had lulled her to sleep and now she peered out of the window at a darkening sky. The ghostly silhouettes of trees rushed past them. The compartment was empty except for her and the professor, who had also taken the opportunity to nod off, his head bent forward.

Adeline returned her attention to her limited view of the outside world. The sky had taken on a greenish hue that reminded her of the house she had fled from. A shudder quickened her muscles.

Bang! A searing flash of light. The carriage lurched forward, backward. Iron scraped against iron. Professor Mayer cried out as he was tossed from his seat.

"My God. Professor. *Professor.*"

Adeline struggled to reach him as the train veered from side to side, throwing her one way and then the other. The professor lay on the floor where he had landed, apparently unconscious. Adeline crawled on all fours and managed to get to him before being thrown aside by the violent motion of the train. The sickening grating of the wheels, the eye-watering smoke that stank and made her throat clench, and, above it all, the screams and cries of the injured and dying. This must be what hell was like. Flashes of light pierced the semi-darkness of the compartment as the train blundered on. Adeline stretched out her hand to the professor. She grabbed his wrist and felt for a pulse, finding nothing. But it couldn't end like this. The professor mustn't die. They still had a job to do.

"Professor, wake up. *Please.*" She gripped the edge of the seat to hoist herself up, fighting against the momentum of the shuddering train.

One massive jolt. Thunderous crashes. Adeline twisted her knee. Daggers of pain shot up her leg—so fierce she couldn't breathe. Trees scraped the window. The train must have left the tracks. Adeline struggled to stand. She must get the professor up on the seat. But then the world seemed to somersault. Her head banged against the carriage wall, and she passed out.

"Madame! Madame!"

Someone shook her arm. Shouted in her ear. Adeline struggled to open her eyes and winced at the bright light. She looked up ...at the floor...

"*Gott sei Dank!* She is alive." A young man in a uniform she didn't recognize bent over her.

"What happened?" Someone must have stuffed her head full of cotton wool. Everything sounded muffled. She moved and pain sliced through her arms and legs. A ferocious headache throbbed at her temples.

The young man came into focus, his kind, brown eyes showing concern while he gently examined her for broken bones.

"There was an explosion. We think a group of nationalists set a bomb on the track. It's a miracle not more people were killed." He laid her arm down gently on her stomach. "You have been very lucky. I can't find any fractures, but we will take you to hospital to be on the safe side. I'm afraid you will be black and blue for a while."

He held up some of his fingers in front of her. "How many do you see?"

"Three," she said.

"Good."

Adeline remembered. "My companion. Professor Mayer. Is he all right?"

The young man's face darkened. "I am so sorry."

Adeline struggled up. Nearby, two of the young man's colleagues were preparing to lift a body, shrouded in a blanket.

"Oh no. Please tell me he's not…"

"I'm afraid so. There was nothing we could do. He was already dead when we got here."

Adeline remembered. "Please. I must… He is carrying something I need to take with me. In his pocket."

The men stopped. One of them reached under the blanket and felt around. He withdrew his hand, laid down a clean handkerchief and some keys. He then repeated the motions.

"That is all there is," he said.

"No, it must be there. A little statue. It is terribly important I have it."

"I'm sorry, madame. It is not here."

Adeline tried to stand. The young man who had been helping her assisted her. Fresh waves of pain shot through her feet and legs and even though he had a gentle touch, her arm throbbed where he held it to steady her.

A rush of cold air from the smashed carriage windows chilled her.

"His briefcase. The professor's briefcase. It must be here."

The men looked around the small compartment.

"It must have been blown out during the crash," the young man said. "But I've found this. It was wedged between the seats or you would have lost it as well." He handed Adeline her purse containing some money, personal items and her house keys. She took it and thanked him.

Panic filled her head and overwhelmed the pain of her bruised limbs. She didn't have the statue and she didn't have the scroll. There was no longer any point in continuing to Taposiris Magna and, in any case, the thought of traveling there alone was unthinkable. She didn't speak the language. She would be a woman alone in a strange country. Who knew what might happen?

But with the statue missing, what did that mean for the future?

All she could do was pray that they had left the evil behind in a basement in Vienna. God protect anyone who came across it.

Dust, grime, manure, and gasoline fumes had turned the air rank, but Adeline wanted to kneel down and kiss the filthy London streets. She had arrived home after more than two weeks in a Trieste hospital, dusty from her journey and distinctly lacking in baggage. The luggage van had gone up in flames. All she possessed was contained in a Gladstone bag a nurse at the hospital in Trieste had given her, along with some serviceable, but not particularly fashionable, clothes to see her through until she could be reunited with her much-depleted wardrobe. Adeline didn't care. Inside her house, she bent to pick up the accumulated mail. She recognized the handwriting on one envelope and ripped it open. A letter from an intrigued Miss Sinclair.

> *My dear Mrs. Ogilvy,*
>
> *What a trying and traumatic time you must have had. You mustn't think of trying to work until you are fully recovered, but I must tell you a quite extraordinary thing happened today…*
>
> Adeline checked the postmark. Two days earlier.
>
> *… An invoice I submitted to Dr. Quintillus's legal firm came back undelivered. I decided to investigate further and went to the address, only to discover that the company had simply closed down. Disappeared. Not even a plaque on the door to show they had ever been there. While I was in the building, I spoke to staff at a few other companies who had offices there and they all said the same thing. None of them had ever heard of Marchant, Finch and Stafford—the legal firm I have been corresponding with until now and who have been paying for your services. They suggested the firm had been using that address purely for receipt of their mail. But what do you think about that? I have never heard of a legal firm without a proper office. Of course, I shall ensure you are paid until the end of the month and look forward to seeing you when you are quite recovered from your ordeal.*

Yours sincerely
Emily Sinclair

Adeline folded the letter and stuffed it back in the envelope. She had half-expected this news—or something like it. In the circumstances, how could such a legal firm exist? Not for the first time since the train crash, Adeline's eyes teared up. If only Professor Mayer were still alive, he would no doubt have a perfectly rational explanation.

She sighed, put the rest of the mail on her kitchen table and drew back the curtains. The sun was shining in Wimbledon. Storm clouds might be gathering across Europe but here, at least for now, she could enjoy the peace and tranquility of an English spring, while her body and her mind healed.

———

Two weeks earlier, on a wrecked railroad track not far from Trieste, a young, smartly dressed man inspected the carnage of twisted iron, smashed, and burned-out carriages and an exploded engine. The fifty-two dead bodies had been removed, but the lingering stench of oil, coal, and charcoal remained. Streaks and pools of congealed blood stained the tracks. Fallen branches and uprooted trees littered the ground beyond, where the front half of the train had toppled over and come to rest. Count Wilhelm von Königsberg shook out the gleaming white handkerchief from his top pocket and held it in front of his nose. The scent of lavender did its best to overpower the noxious odors.

He caught a gleam of metal and stepped carefully over a bent and twisted rail. With his gloved hand, he prodded the gold object and pulled it out. Filthy and covered in grease it might be but what a few wipes of his handkerchief revealed spread a smile across his face. Irina would love this. She never ceased to tell him how much she admired Egyptian art.

The once-pristine handkerchief was ruined forever as he wrapped the precious statue and placed it in the pocket of his top coat. No one had seen him. They were all too busy. This would be a major salvage operation and his father's company stood to make a small fortune. One day he would inherit it all. One day he and Irina would be independently wealthy. And if war did come, as his father predicted, that day could come much sooner than anyone yet anticipated.

Wilhelm looked around. Maybe he could find more where that little statue had come from. Strange how it had felt when he held it. Energy surged within it and seeped through his now-filthy glove and into his veins.

A battered briefcase lay a few yards away, half-hidden in the debris at the side of the track. Closer inspection revealed that half of it had burned almost to charcoal, and its contents were scorched and unidentifiable. That was about as far as the fire had extended. As a result, around two hundred passengers escaped with their lives.

Satisfied that there were no other trinkets of interest, Wilhelm went back to the business of the day. How to ensure maximum profit from the devastation all around him.

In his pocket, the statue lay, quietly gleaming. Gold and green.

Part Two
1923

Chapter 14

Hietzing, Vienna

Wilhelm discovered the entrance to the basement from the library a few days after he and Irina moved in. He wasn't a great reader and the library's only fascination for him had been in the Klimt ceiling which looked in need of some urgent attention. A sunny day, with light streaming in through the large windows had enticed him over to the far side of the room for the first time. He gazed out across the overgrown garden and decided to employ a gardener.

He was turning away when he spotted the inconspicuous handle. The key was in the lock.

Curiosity led him onward. A fusty smell of disuse hit him and he wrinkled his nose. He searched in vain for a light switch and made another mental note. He must get an electrician in.

He looked around the library and spotted an oil lamp on the partner desk. He removed the glass funnel and lit the wick. Once he had adjusted the flame to his liking, he took the lamp and made his careful way down the steps.

Wilhelm reached another closed door at the end of the corridor. He turned the handle and pushed. The hinges creaked a little, but nothing a drop of oil wouldn't cure.

Once inside, he shone the lamp around the still, quiet room.

The red hieroglyphics grabbed his attention.

They've been written in blood. He dismissed the thought and shook his head. The room was a little spooky. Weren't all basements? He stared at the symbols for a minute and wished he could understand what they meant. He turned back to face the rest of the room. A short distance away, the floor seemed darker. Wilhelm moved toward the patch and bent down. Small piles of charcoal-colored ash lay scattered across a couple of square feet of stone floor. He picked up a little in his fingers and rubbed them together. Maybe someone had been burning old papers, but the texture seemed wrong somehow. The residue clung to his fingers in an unpleasant, almost greasy fashion.

He rested the lamp on the floor while he rubbed his hands on a handkerchief. Then he picked up the lamp and stood. A glint of gold in the light sent shivers coursing through his body. A portrait of a woman…her profile looked familiar, although he couldn't think when he would have met such an exotic creature. Besides, this one must be an Egyptian queen. Cleopatra. Or Nefertiti maybe? No. Cleopatra. He spotted a signature. He peered closer and nearly dropped the lamp. What in God's name was an original Klimt doing down in a dingy basement room?

The excitement was almost too much to bear. He must tell Irina. After all, she… He started toward the door and then stopped. No. Not yet. Not until he could show it to her in all its glory. First there must be light. And due ceremony. In the fullness of time, the portrait must hang in the library. He'd rename it the Klimt Room and take great delight in showing it off to his friends. But for now, let it stay here, surrounded by those hieroglyphics and, of course he had his own Egyptian artifact. The little gold statuette he had found all those years ago, when he and Irina were first married, graced the mantelpiece upstairs. He had put it there himself this very morning.

He would bring it down here. Just for the unveiling to Irina. Until then, not a word.

He moved closer to the portrait and shone the light closer to it, then moved to one side. Still it seemed to focus on him. He moved to the other side. Then a bit farther away, until he could barely see the features himself. No matter which way he turned, her gaze followed him. But then, Gustav Klimt was a most talented portrait painter. His early death, in 1918, had been a great loss to the art world and beyond.

A sudden cold draft disturbed his train of thought. It seemed to come from within the room itself, but that wasn't possible. Had he imagined the slight fluttering of the pile of ash? No, it had definitely moved. He couldn't see where his fingers had left indentations when he had picked some of it up.

It must have come from the door. But that was on the opposite side of the room from the direction he had felt it.

Wilhelm shrugged. No matter. As he had thought earlier, basements were always a bit spooky, and this one was no exception.

Sighing, reluctant to leave the portrait, he nevertheless left the room and closed the creaking door behind him.

Back in the library, he closed and locked the basement entrance. He hesitated and then removed the little key, placing it in his waistcoat pocket. Wouldn't do for Irina to discover this and go down before he'd got her surprise ready for her.

"I'm telling you, there's something not right down there in your basement." The wretched-looking electrician was wringing his cloth cap in his trembling hands.

Wilhelm studied him with contempt. This silly little man was ruining all his plans for Irina's surprise. If he didn't finish the job in the next day or two, she would be bound to become suspicious. She was already asking some awkward questions, such as why this workman had run out of their home white-faced and screaming that he'd seen some sort of ghost in the basement. It didn't help either that their eccentric housekeeper kept filling her head with old superstitions about the house and its former owner.

"I suppose this is all a ruse to squeeze more money out of me."

The man looked horrified. "No, sir, I can assure you it wouldn't matter how much money you offered me, I wouldn't go back down in that basement. I would never go back down there. What I saw there... No man should ever have to see that. Nor woman come to that."

Furious, Wilhelm threw his half-smoked cigarette into the fire. "I contracted you to complete a job for me. Electricity. In the basement. You will not get a single krone out of me until the job is completed."

"But sir! I have completed the kitchen and the wine cellar. I have expenses..."

Wilhelm's lips twisted into an unpleasant grimace. "Then you had better set to and fulfil your contract, hadn't you? And you had best be quick about it if you don't want your children to go hungry." Wilhelm turned his back on the hapless electrician who hesitated for a few moments and then sped out of the library. He never returned.

Two days later, Wilhelm managed to engage another electrician. This one came from out of town—from a small village in Lower Austria where, presumably, the errant workman's lurid tales of ghosts in the basement had not reached.

He worked quickly and, a couple of days later, he managed to stutter that he had completed the job.

Wilhelm noted the man's shaking hands and frowned. What was it about the laboring class? No doubt the man had been drinking beer in a local hostelry and had been regaled with gossip about the Königsberg House.

"I shall inspect your work and if I am satisfied I shall pay you today."

The man nodded. "I can promise you, you won't be unhappy. I take a pride in my work. All my customers know that."

The man was gabbling. He seemed ill at ease and a long way from the confident, almost cocky, young man who had taken on the job.

"Come along then," Wilhelm said. He strode across the room.

"Oh, I'd as soon wait up here if you don't mind."

"I do mind. Come with me. Show me where the switches are."

"You can't miss them. They're—"

"I said, come with me. If you wish to be paid, that is."

Incredibly to Wilhelm, the man actually seemed to be weighing up which course of action to take. Wilhelm stood by the entrance to the basement, tapping his foot.

Eventually the man shrugged, inhaled deeply and joined him.

The electrician led the way. He practically raced down the steps, as if he couldn't wait to be done and out of there.

He waved his arms, pointing out switches on the walls and throwing each one in turn, so that light flooded from the overhead bulbs.

Finally, they stood in front of the portrait. "So, you see sir, I have done exactly as you asked me. Could you pay me now, sir, please?"

"My goodness, you are in a hurry. What is your rush?" Wilhelm's eyes were riveted by the portrait, revealed in light that made the gold gleam and her eye shine with violet fire.

"I...I would really like to get off now, sir. If you don't mind."

Wilhelm reached into his pocket and pulled out a wodge of notes. He peeled off a few and counted them out into the electrician's shaking hands.

"I believe that is the sum we agreed."

"Yes, sir. Thank you, sir. I'll be off then."

"Yes, yes, away you go then." Wilhelm made a shooing gesture with his hand and the man scurried away as if a demon were after him.

A sudden cold draft wafted through the room.

Just like before.

An audible, deep sigh. The hairs on Wilhelm's neck prickled.

I'm becoming as fanciful as that damned electrician. I'll be imagining I'm hearing voices or seeing strange men with long hair in top hats like his predecessor.

Wilhelm smiled at the portrait. She seemed so real. She looked like she could have spoken if she had chosen to.

"But you won't, will you?" he said to her. "Or you'll have me charging out of here like those workmen." He laughed and thought he heard an echoed response.

I'm letting the atmosphere down here get to me.

Reluctantly, he tore himself away but, in that second, he could have sworn he saw the face turn, ever so slightly. He stared hard, but the profile remained, exactly as it should be. Static in its frame.

Wilhelm looked briefly for the pile of ash, but it had been scattered thinly across the floor, probably by the heavy boots of the electricians. No matter, the room could do with a damn good clean anyway. He'd tell the housekeeper to send one of the maids to do it.

He stepped out into the corridor and flicked off the light switch. He turned...a sudden icy blast, and the door slammed in his face.

Puzzled, he hurried back up to the library and, once again, turned the key in the lock, surprised at how his hand shook.

A tray containing brandy, a glass, and a jug of water stood on an occasional table by the fireplace. Today was too warm for the fire to be lit, but Wilhelm felt chilled throughout his body. He sloshed brandy into the glass, reached for the water, changed his mind, and downed the neat spirit in one gulp. The fiery liquid burned away the chill and soothed his anxiety. He smiled while he refilled his glass. One day he and Irina would have a good laugh about this. After she'd seen the portrait of course.

"Irina, you simply *must* come down here. You'll *love* this room."

Irina von Königsberg hesitated at the top of the stairs leading from the library to the basement. Her husband's handsome face smiled up at her from the entrance to the room beyond. "Now we've got electric light down here, it's amazing. The hieroglyphics…and there's a wonderful portrait. Looks like it could be of Cleopatra. It's by Gustav Klimt for heaven's sake. What on earth it's doing down here, goodness only knows. I'll bring it up later and it can hang in the library. It'll look wonderful there with that ceiling. Oh, *do* come and see, Irina."

"I don't like cellars. They're so….so…" Even after ten years, Irina still found German a trial. The temptation to lapse into her native Russian pulled at her, but Wilhelm wouldn't approve, and, in any case, his Russian was basic at best. She stroked her fashionably shingled black hair and found the word she was looking for.

"Creepy. They are too creepy. I think a ghost might leap out at me."

Her husband, Wilhelm, let out a bellow of laughter. "Oh, Irina, you beautiful goose. The only thing that's going to leap out at you will be me."

Irina put the toe of her expensive, silk-covered shoe on the top step and bit her lip. "If you are sure it is safe."

"Of course it is, you silly thing. You've been listening to too many of the housekeeper's stories."

Irina clung to the handrail while she made her uncertain descent. "I think they are not silly stories. I think these things happened."

At the foot of the stairs, she took her husband's hand and he led her into the room. She gasped at the red-painted hieroglyphics adorning the wall. Then she caught her breath at the sight of the portrait. Below it, on a purple-draped altar, stood the small gold statue Wilhelm had given her ten years earlier.

"Why do you bring that down here? It belongs in the library."

"I borrowed it from there to put it with all the other Egyptian stuff in here. It looks right, doesn't it? Anyway, once I remove the portrait and take it up to the library, it could hang above the fireplace and the statue could stand on the mantel below it."

Irina caught Wilhelm staring at her intently. It made her uncomfortable. Everything about this room made her nerve-ends prickle.

The hairs on the back of Irina's neck stood and goosebumps erupted along her arms. A breeze wafted over her. She could have sworn she'd heard the lightest of whispers. A woman's voice speaking in a strange tongue. She shook her head. Cellars *were* creepy. She'd said so herself. And she probably *had* been listening a little too much to that strange housekeeper's stories.

The woman had come with the house and Irina hadn't the heart to throw her out when they moved in. She'd told them she had lived all alone in the increasingly derelict mansion since before the war and, besides, she was efficient and hardworking. The house was beautiful again and the woman proved herself dedicated to keeping it that way, but that didn't make her any less odd. The way her eyes would seem to lose focus, as if she saw something no one else could...

Wilhelm still gazed intently at her. Irina felt self-conscious and touched her hair again, but every single strand was securely in place, forming a modish glossy black helmet. Still, there had to be a reason for her husband's intense gaze.

"Why are you staring at me like that?" she asked.

"It's quite remarkable. You didn't pose for that portrait by any chance, did you?"

"Of course not."

"You must admit, she is the image of you. It makes me wonder if your family's stories are true after all. Maybe you *are* related to Cleopatra."

This time she knew it was real. The breeze even ruffled her hair and, judging by the way he flinched, Wilhelm also appeared to have felt it.

"Is it my imagination or has it grown much colder in here?" he asked.

The woman's voice startled them. "You are not imagining it." She stood in the entrance. "It would have been better for you never to have come to this place."

Irina and Wilhelm stared at their housekeeper, who glared at them.

Irina moistened her lips. "What have you done to yourself?"

Gone was the housekeeper's demure black dress and tidy bun. She had arranged her hair in a cluster of tight, long braids and dressed in a long, white sheath dress. Her eyes were heavily outlined in kohl.

Irina stared at her and repeated her question. "What have you done to yourself?"

The woman shook her head. "If you had possessed the scroll, you would have known. You have brought the statue back here. Her tomb dust is also here— in the oil paint of the portrait." She pointed at the picture. "The statue and her remains, when present together, are a force more powerful than you can imagine. What is to be done, will be done. I cannot help you." She turned and left the stunned couple.

Irina and Wilhelm stared after her, too stunned to speak. Finally, Irina broke the silence. "What is she talking about? What scroll?"

Wilhelm shrugged. "I have no idea."

The lights dimmed until a mere glow illuminated the room. It cast deep shadows. On the far wall, a shape emerged.

Irina screamed and pointed. "What is that?"

The tall figure moved forward.

"His eyes!" Irina collapsed against her husband, who clung to her, unable to make his legs work.

The hideous intruder's mouth opened and words hissed from within. He spoke in perfect, but brittle German. "Let her go. She is mine now."

"Irina is my wife."

"She is my beloved queen. Reborn. You have brought the statue of Set back to its rightful place, to be with the essence of my queen."

A sickening crack of dry bones. The man—if he was a man—turned his head toward the painting.

Bile shot up into Irina's throat. Her head buzzed and she struggled to remain conscious. She clung tighter to Wilhelm.

His voice trembled as he spoke. "Who…who are you?"

"Dr. Emeryk Quintillus. This is my house."

"But I…" Wilhelm stopped.

"You have the scroll?" Quintillus asked.

"What scroll? We know nothing about a scroll."

Quintillus couldn't be staring at them. The black holes in his head where his eyes should have been told her that. Yet Irina was certain he *could* see them and that, right now, he was staring at them keenly, searching for any sign they might be lying.

"All is told in the scroll, but it is incomplete. If it were not, I should not be in this…condition. But all will be well now I have the statue—and the portrait."

Again the awful cracking of those dry bones as he turned his head—this time to stare at the picture.

Irina cried out.

The figure in the portrait moved. Almost dissolved, only to re-emerge full face. The kohl-rimmed dark eyes stared outward, unblinking, as if painted that way. The lips were set in a haughty, regal pose, but nevertheless appeared full, moist and sensual. Now Irina knew why Wilhelm had stared at her so intently. She could have posed for that portrait.

Quintillus looked from the picture to the woman and back again. "Soon you will return, my queen. Soon we will be together and I shall be reborn."

Wilhelm clung to Irina. "This is my wife. She is not yours to take."

Quintillus raised his hand to strike out but lowered it again. A slight smile turned up the corners of his lips and a green glow began to pulsate and grow. It cloaked the portrait.

The portrait shook violently and suddenly crashed to the floor, shattering the frame. The paint began to run and separate. Gray dust collected in a pile.

A gust of wind whipped up around Irina. It knocked Wilhelm across the room and swept her up. She fought against it before it hurled her against the wall.

Quintillus's voice echoed around the room. "Come to me, my beloved queen. Come to me, Cleopatra."

The statue of Set glowed. The sound of a woman chanting filled the small room. Irina's lips moved. Still unconscious, she took up the chant.

Quintillus writhed, every movement creaking and rustling. The dust from the painting swirled into a tornado. Some rained down on him. He slammed his hands against his face and toppled forward. He fell to his knees.

Wilhelm struggled to get to his feet, but some unseen force held him there. His arms and legs refused to obey him.

Quintillus's hands changed. No longer withered and dry, they pulsed with life. Fresh skin spread in a clear pink wave. Veins flowed with life-giving blood.

More dust rained down—this time on Irina, instantly absorbed by her skin and through her silk dress. She stirred, opened her mouth and spoke. Words Wilhelm didn't understand. In a language he had never heard before. She opened her eyes and stared straight through her husband. Her lip curled. Unintelligible anger spewed from her lips.

Wilhelm's tears poured down his face. "*Irina*. Forgive me. I didn't know!"

Irina shut her eyes and slumped forward.

Quintillus removed his hands from his face and stood, staggering a little. Wilhelm stared at the hate-filled dark eyes, newly emerged from the empty sockets.

The force that had held him fast released Wilhelm and he took an uncertain step toward his unconscious wife. Quintillus reached into the inside pocket of his jacket.

"I want my wife," Wilhelm said, making another move.

Quintillus opened his mouth and let out a guffaw of laughter. "Your wife? Your wife is dead. My beloved queen inhabits her body now."

"You're mad. I don't know what kind of hellish charade is going on here, but you are mad."

Quintillus withdrew his hand from his pocket and pointed the small pistol at Wilhelm's heart.

"Your wife has no further need of you."

One single shot felled Wilhelm. Straight through the heart. Dead.

The woman on the floor stirred. She opened her eyes.

Quintillus knelt before her and took her hand. He placed it to his lips.

"My queen. My beloved."

Cleopatra's eyes focused. She wrenched her hand free, leaped to her feet, then staggered. She appeared uncertain of her new body. She backed away from Quintillus, then spun around. A familiar voice rang out from the corridor.

"I see you are both here," the housekeeper said. "And you have murdered the poor count, Herr Doktor."

"I had no use for him."

"No, of course. And now you believe you have all you desire."

Dr. Quintillus smiled. "I do."

"Such a shame. My sister will never forgive you for what you have done. But you will have time beyond imagining to try to persuade her."

Quintillus's expression darkened. "What do you mean? She is restored, in the body of her descendant. She is born anew. The curse that drained my body of its life has been lifted. All that the scroll described has been fulfilled. We will live together, for eternity."

"No!" Cleopatra lashed out at Quintillus. "What have you done? You have taken me from my resting place. You have taken me from the only man I ever loved."

Quintillus took a step toward her. "My beloved queen. I have waited my whole life to be with you. I have been cursed to walk here these past years, neither dead nor alive. Unable to leave, my only hope that somehow my destiny could still be fulfilled. I took some of the dust from your remains. That much is true."

"You stole the statue of Set from out of my hands, where it lay to give me protection from this." She flung out her arm toward the woman in the doorway. "Arsinoe. My treacherous sister."

Raucous laughter echoed from the woman who stood watching the exchange.

Quintillus took another step closer. "My beloved Cleopatra. Everything I have endured has been for you. I have murdered for you. I forfeited my life for you."

Cleopatra opened her mouth and hissed at him. "You didn't know that would happen. The scroll was damaged. I tore off the last section. You didn't know the spirits of the dead would come to you and drink your blood and drain your body. Tell me, how did it feel to be drunk dry?"

Quintillus shuddered. "Why did you destroy it?"

"To make sure anyone who tried to part me from my beloved Mark Antony would never live to enjoy it."

"Yet here I am, my beloved queen. Restored and whole. For you."

Cleopatra sprang forward and raked her nails down his face. Rivulets of fresh blood streamed down his cheeks. He ignored them and clutched her shoulders. But her strength was unexpected. She wrenched herself free of his grasp.

"You will never possess me. *Never!*"

Arsinoe began a slow handclap.

Cleopatra turned on her sister. "As for you, I curse you. By the power of Set I curse you."

Arsinoe stopped clapping and shook her head. "You cannot curse me, for I am already cursed. Set has heard me. While you held his image in your dead hands, you had his protection. He would do nothing to harm you. Once this man—" she pointed at Quintillus, "—took the statuette away from you, the protection was gone. I could enter from the dark world where my soul has wandered for centuries, waiting for my chance. I should thank the doctor for giving it to me."

Quintillus's hands dropped to his sides.

Arsinoe continued. "Finally, after all these years, justice will be done. At first, I wanted you dead, your soul left to wander among the shades of the soulless for all eternity. But this is a more fitting revenge.

Set will grant my wish and you, dear sister, will be trapped here with a man you do not love. Conscious, alive, but unable to leave this place. Either of you."

"You have not the power," Cleopatra spat the words out.

"What is your intention?" Quintillus demanded. "To trap us here? In this room?"

Arsinoe raised her arm. "Foolish man, meddling with powers you could not comprehend. You deserve your fate almost as much as my sister deserves hers."

A shaft of green light tore through the room and the flickering shadow of Set took substance on the wall where the picture had been. He raised his staff and a beam of hot white light shot out from it. The walls trembled and cracks appeared, scything down the plaster.

Quintillus backed away. Cleopatra stared. Transfixed.

Arsinoe's voice echoed around the room. "I damn you. For all time. You shall have no rest. Not for all eternity. You shall know this hell on earth, as I have known it in the world beyond. The unquiet souls of this house shall be your companions and the man now at your side will never leave you."

Arsinoe left them and walked steadily along the corridor. Behind her, the door slammed. Under her feet, a faint rumbling began and she quickened her step. She must return upstairs now. Set was already hard at work.

She mounted the steps. A long, agonized wail issued from below.

"Arsinoe!"

She paused for a second and smiled. Then hurried up to the library.

She closed the door. It began to seal into a smooth wooden panel. As she watched, the lock and handle disappeared as if they had never been there.

In the room that had been Quintillus's bedroom and in the kitchen, the entrances leading to the basement were obliterated. Only the one in the hall, leading to the kitchen, wine cellar and servants' areas remained.

The house settled into silence. The basement kept its secrets. For now.

Part Three
1964

Chapter 15

The Königsberg House, Hietzing, Vienna

Count Markus von Dürnstein tapped his gold pen against his teeth. "So, there are more rooms down there?"

The fresh-faced young architect he had engaged sat back in his chair in the sumptuous library. He seemed to be trying to contain his excitement, concerned, no doubt, to maintain a professional image in front of this important and influential new client. Markus was used to this. In his position, controlling a number of multi-million-dollar organizations, people tended to tread warily around him. They fought hard for his business. Losing it could have an immediate and detrimental effect on their careers,

Dieter Scheidegger had demonstrated talent and creative flair in the renovation and restoration plans he had designed and carried out for Markus. This latest project—if it was to come off—would be an even bigger commission for him and the company he worked for.

Above the two men, the newly restored Klimt ceiling gleamed with fresh gold leaf. Markus glanced up at it, a fleeting memory of the peeling paint and flaking gold of a few months ago flashed through his mind.

Dieter Scheidegger cleared his throat. "By my estimation, sir, some of the area down there has been sealed off at some point, but so skillfully, it looks like it was constructed that way. At present there is no access, but I'm sure that can be addressed. Of course, in a number of cases, these large houses were constructed with doorways in some of the rooms, and stairs leading down to the bowels of the building. Secret passages if you prefer. But, at present I haven't found any here."

Markus von Dürnstein laid his pen down and sat forward. He rested his elbows on the desk and steepled his fingers. Could he trust this man? It seemed he had little alternative.

"As you know, I inherited this house last year from my uncle, Count Karl von Königsberg. He was a very old man when he died, but he told me the strangest tale once."

The architect's eyebrows raised.

Markus continued. "He said that his younger brother—Wilhelm—and his wife, Irina, bought this place in 1923. The house is named after them. They spoke of finding a strange woman living here at the time, quite unofficially, and taking care of the place. They took pity on her and employed her as their housekeeper. One day, Wilhelm told my Uncle Karl about a fantastic room he had found in the basement, complete with a previously unknown portrait by Gustav Klimt. Soon after that though, Wilhelm, Irina, and the housekeeper all disappeared and were never seen again. Neither my uncle nor I have ever been able to locate the room Wilhelm spoke of. I will confess I had even begun to consider that my uncle might have imagined it all, but it has always seemed odd that the kitchen and service areas below stairs take up so little floor space relative to the size of the building."

The architect nodded. "That was my first thought. I felt certain there had to be more, but it was certainly well hidden. That is a fantastic story, though. Imagine if we were to drill through and find that room. It would be a little like Howard Carter discovering the tomb of Tutankhamen. Without the curse. Or the body, of course!" The architect laughed.

A cold chill spread over Markus. "Indeed, I fervently hope we do not encounter any such things. My relations were not the only ones to go missing from this house. Some years earlier two men reported the disappearance of their sister—a woman called Magda Varga, a maid here at the time. She was never found." Markus glanced at his watch. He had a meeting with his accountant in an hour.

"How strange," Dieter Scheidegger said. "Well, I certainly hope we don't find her." He laughed and gathered his plans together which he pushed into his briefcase. He stood. "I mustn't take up any more of your time this morning, sir." He extended his hand. "Thank you for seeing me. I shall look forward to working with you again."

Markus stood and shook his hand. "Thank you for coming, Magister Scheidegger. I shall look forward to discussing this in more detail when you have some costings for me."

"Within the week." The architect shook Markus's hand.

After he had left, Markus sat down and tapped his pen against his teeth again, then stopped when he realized he was doing it. An annoying habit that had crept up on him a couple of years ago. Try as he might he couldn't break it.

He hoped he was doing the right thing by making these alterations. After all, if that room really did exist, there was a potentially valuable Klimt that no one even knew existed, hanging there on a damp wall, gathering dust. Markus was enough of an admirer of the painter to have his curiosity spiked by the prospect of finding such a treasure. As far as he knew, there were no other missing Klimt pictures. All the others were present and accounted for, either in public or private ownership. Like his ceiling. The thousands of schillings he had spent on restoration had been well worth the investment.

Markus von Dürnstein was not an extravagant man, but he never balked at paying for quality. No doubt this hidden painting — assuming it did exist — would also require restoration but, when and if the time came, he wouldn't hesitate.

He set his pen down neatly in front of him and pushed his chair back. Straightening his jacket, he strode out into the hall. In the kitchen, the cook nearly dropped her mixing bowl.

"Oh, sir, we weren't expecting you." She adjusted her snow-white cap and the kitchen maid curtseyed. The butler appeared from the direction of the wine cellar. All eyes were on their employer, who never ventured below stairs.

"Sorry to disturb you all, but I understand my architect has been down here, investigating the possible existence of some other rooms."

The butler cleared his throat. Leichner was a well-built man in his fifties with a bullet head and an unparalleled knowledge of vintage wine. He was also unimaginative and, in the eight years he had been in

Markus's employ, the count couldn't remember him cracking even a slight smile. But between him and the housekeeper, Frau Palfry, the household ran smoothly.

"Leichner, will you show me where the architect has been concentrating his efforts?"

The butler inclined his head slightly. "Certainly, sir. This way please."

Markus followed him past the wine cellar and the butler's pantry. Ahead of him was a plastered wall punctured by some drill holes.

"Here, sir. Magister Scheidegger brought a man with him. A short man with a rather large and noisy drill."

Markus leaned forward and peered closely at the holes. They were of a very small circumference. No doubt that would ensure minimum defacing of the wall before a decision had been made whether or not to demolish it.

Markus poked at one of the holes. A slight draft tickled his finger.

"Looks as if the architect was correct. There is something in there. Another room. Maybe more."

Leichner stepped back. He looked like something had struck him.

"What's the matter?" Markus asked.

The butler shook his head. A little too vigorously. He was hiding something. But Markus let it drop. He had bigger things on his mind.

"I'm afraid this work is going to mean an awful lot of disruption for you and the staff," he said. "And a lot of dust and plaster when this wall comes down. I trust you will all be able to cope?"

"Oh yes, sir. I plan to seal this part of the basement off. We can hang some old sheets, and the servants and I will arrange it so that the workmen carry out their tasks behind them. In that way, we can minimize the amount of dust and dirt."

"Perhaps make sure they take their dirty boots off before they traipse through the kitchen." Markus smiled. He had never doubted Leichner would have already thought the scheme through. Butlers like him were worth the higher-than-average salary he was paying the man.

A sigh drifted along the corridor. To his amazement, Markus saw his stoic butler flinch. His face paled and his top lip trembled.

"Leichner, whatever's the matter?"

"N…nothing, sir. Only a draft I expect."

An uneasy sensation passed through Markus. The second time in almost as few minutes he had felt certain his butler knew something he didn't. This time he wouldn't let it pass.

"Something's happened, Leichner, and I want you to tell me what it is. Good God, man, I've never seen you like this. You're shaking."

The butler seemed to consider this for a moment. But his profound sense of duty to his employer must have overcome his clear desire to say nothing. "Yes, sir. But, please, not here."

The man looked absolutely terrified.

"Very well, come up to the library."

Markus led his butler back through the kitchen, ignoring the bemused expression on the cook's face.

Up in the library, Leichner stood in front of Markus who sat at the desk.

"Right, Leichner, out with it. What has put you in this state?"

Leichner's Adam's apple wobbled. He swallowed hard. "Before I answer you, sir, I must stress that I am not, by nature, a fanciful man."

"I am aware of that. You are probably the last person I would ever describe as fanciful."

"You will understand, sir, that for me to say what I am about to say is only because I have witnessed it with my own eyes. Otherwise, I should never have believed it."

"Witnessed what, Leichner?"

"Sir…it all started when the drilling began last week. Until then, nothing strange or peculiar ever occurred downstairs, but a few hours after the workman left, I happened to be in the wine cellar checking the stock. I felt a slight draft on the back of my neck. Soft. As if someone had breathed on me. It took me by surprise, sir, and I immediately turned round to see who it was. I thought it might be the new maid and was ready to admonish her. But it wasn't…" His voice faltered. The color had drained from his face.

"Go on, Leichner. Tell me. If it wasn't the girl, who was it?"

"No one. At least…at least no one…human."

"What? What do you mean, 'no one human'? An animal of some kind? Do we have rats down there?"

"Oh, how I wish it were that simple. No, sir, we do not have rats, and no, it wasn't any animal. I saw a shadow. An impossible shadow. Only for an instant that time. It flashed past, near where I stood. I saw a man in a tall hat… Sir, I realize how this must sound."

Markus tried to take it all in. Had his butler experienced some kind of brainstorm? He certainly looked sincere. He must believe it himself. Surely Leichner lacked the imagination to invent something like this. Maybe he should call on the services of a psychiatrist. Perhaps the man had been working too hard. Markus could send him away to his country home in Styria for a few weeks. The clean rural air would set him to rights and put all this nonsense out of his head.

"Leichner. I realize such an experience would be highly unnerving and disorientating for you. The brain is a strange organ. It does so much for us, but in times of stress it can also turn on us. Make us believe things we know cannot be true and imagine things that aren't there. When did you last take a vacation? I certainly can't remember you taking more than the odd day here and there." Thinking about it, Markus couldn't remember a single year when his butler had taken any significant amount of time off.

The butler shifted his weight from one foot to the other. "I know what I have said must sound impossible. I tried to dismiss it, too. Some kind of optical illusion. A trick of the light—"

"Precisely."

"I almost managed to convince myself. But then I saw it again. And this time, I have no doubt in my mind that what I witnessed was actually there."

Markus's relief evaporated.

His initial reluctance gone, the butler seemed anxious to pour all his experiences out in some sort of cathartic tidal wave. Markus could only sit and listen, growing increasingly concerned about his butler's mental state.

"It was yesterday. Once again, I had gone down into the wine cellar. Just as before, I heard a sigh and felt a draft on my neck. This time, I moved quicker. I spun around and saw the shadow pass out of the room. I dashed out into the corridor and saw the man, as clear as I can see you. He was tall, dressed in a top hat of the sort that American

President wore. Lincoln. He wore a long, old-fashioned jacket and his hair was so long, it seemed halfway down his back. He stopped. Maybe he had heard me. I froze on the spot, and I don't mind telling you sir that it was through sheer terror. I knew this man couldn't be human. Maybe he had never been human. And the smell. As if something had died long ago and never been buried. Then he turned around. His eyes bored into me. His face was deathly white…at least the part not covered by a beard. His lips were set firm. I don't know how long we stood there. He stood some yards away, a few feet from the wall that is to come down. Then, he seemed to fade. He went from a solid form to a shadowy mist in a few seconds. Then the mist disappeared through the drill holes and was gone. I tell you, sir, it was a few minutes before I could breathe normally again. Even longer before I trusted myself to walk away from there."

Markus blinked and tried to sort out his jumbled thoughts. What should he do about this? His butler was clearly having some kind of a mental breakdown. Maybe the vacation in Styria would be a first resort. If that didn't set him to rights, then medical help would have to be sought.

"Have you told anyone else about this? Frau Palfry for example?"

The butler shook his head. "No, sir, you are the only one I have told, and I wouldn't have mentioned it to you but for what happened down there. Whatever it is has been let into this house by that drilling. I implore you, sir, don't fetch that wall down. Seal up those holes. The rest of the basement was sealed up for a reason and it needs to stay that way."

Markus wouldn't have been surprised if Leichner hadn't sunk to his knees, so anxious were his pleas. He must convince the butler to take the vacation he so desperately needed.

"I appreciate your dedication to your job and your hard work and untiring efforts on my behalf, Leichner, but I must be a responsible employer here. I can see you are tired and exhausted. You haven't taken a proper vacation in years, and I am telling you to take a month off on full pay. You can travel to my house near Trautenfels. You have been there on a number of occasions when you have accompanied me. I believe you have enjoyed the beautiful scenery and countryside?"

"Yes, indeed, sir, it is very beautiful, but—"

"No 'buts', Leichner. I will not take a refusal from you. You need a vacation. I blame myself entirely. I should have seen this coming. I know you take a great pride in your work, but Frau Palfry is very capable. She will run things in your absence and when you come back, refreshed and clear-minded once more, you will be able to take charge again."

Far from showing any pleasure or gratitude, Leichner looked even more shaken and desperate. "But, sir, I implore you, please don't go ahead with this work. You'll unleash untold evil into this house. There's something behind that wall that should never be allowed out of there."

Markus moved out from behind the desk and pushed the bell on the wall near the fireplace.

"Go and pack your suitcase, Leichner. I will instruct Frau Palfry to tell Schmidt to drive you in my car." Leichner opened his mouth to speak once more. "No, I will hear no more of this. Go and pack your suitcase. You will leave within the hour. Enjoy your vacation. You have well and truly earned it. I will inform the staff at Trautenfels to expect you and to grant your every wish as if it were my own."

Leichner had sufficient experience to recognize when he was defeated. He lowered his head.

"Yes, sir. Thank you, sir."

He turned to go as Frau Palfry entered the room. She frowned at Leichner's expression. Clearly, she wasn't used to seeing the butler in this condition, either.

After he had told her of Leichner's imminent departure for his vacation, Markus asked her, "Have you seen or heard anything strange since the drilling began?"

Frau Palfry's eyes widened. By her expression, she seemed to be wondering if her employer had experienced some kind of blow to the head.

"No, sir, nothing out of the ordinary."

Markus smiled in what he hoped was a reassuring way. "That's fine, Frau Palfry. Thank you, I'm sure my house is in safe hands while

Leichner is enjoying his vacation. His first proper one since entering my employ I believe?"

"Well, I don't know about that, but I have been here six years and he has never taken more than three days off at a time. He doesn't have any family, you see sir. I suppose he doesn't really have anywhere to go or anyone to go with."

"So, high time he did have a break."

"Yes, sir. He works very hard."

"Indeed, Frau Palfry. As you do yourself. Thank you."

Frau Palfry inclined her head slightly and left.

Markus was satisfied he had done right by his butler, but a growing sense of unease kept him awake that night, along with a memory.

When he had been down there with the butler, examining the holes made by the drill, they had both felt the same draft at the same time. The draft that had led his butler to turn whiter than Markus's bed linen. And the butler had described a noxious smell of something long dead. That same smell had floated briefly into Markus's own nostrils. And it had come from beyond the wall.

Chapter 16

Markus crossed the hall on his way out to dinner. He never made it.

Frau Palfry's scream stopped him dead.

He tore down the back stairs to find the terrified housekeeper, sobbing and shaking, being comforted by the cook and the new maid.

"Whatever is all this noise about?" Markus said.

Frau Palfry choked back her sobs. All eyes turned to him.

The cook spoke. "I'm sorry, sir, Frau Palfry saw something in the corridor where all the work's going on. It frightened her."

Markus kept his voice calm. He took the housekeeper's trembling hands in his. "What did you see there?"

Frau Palfry raised her tear-stained face to his. Her eyes were red from weeping but wild and terrified. She shook her head, slightly at first, then vigorously.

Markus tried again. Unease built up in his stomach. "It's all right, you can tell me."

"I...I...c-can't."

"Yes, you can. Tell me. Don't be afraid. There's nothing to be afraid of."

She wrenched one hand free and pointed behind her without turning around. "Down there. Something...unnatural." She swayed and Markus caught her before she fell in a dead faint.

The cook and the maid helped to get her to a chair, where they positioned her with her head between her knees. Within seconds she was coming to. She sat up and put her hands to each side of her head. "Buzzing."

"I'll get you some brandy, Frau Palfry," the cook said, and seemed grateful for something to do.

"Not cooking brandy," Markus said, "The good stuff. There's a case of Remy Martin in the wine cellar." He fished his keys out of his pocket and indicated the correct one to the cook. She hesitated for a moment and then hurried away.

Less than a minute later, Frau Palfry opened her eyes. An earsplitting scream issued from the corridor, along with the sound of someone running as if their life depended on it.

The cook raced into the kitchen, clutching a bottle of cognac in one hand and her chest with the other, her face ashen.

"Whatever's the matter?" Markus asked. His heart beat quicker and the growing fear coalesced into something approaching terror.

He took the bottle from the cook's trembling hands and set it down on the nearby table.

The cook made an obvious effort to control herself sufficiently to speak, while Frau Palfry gazed straight ahead, a glazed expression on her face.

"I saw…what she must have seen." She pointed at Frau Palfry. "A man. A horrible, unnatural man. He came through the curtain."

"In front of the demolished wall?"

The cook nodded.

"Then I must investigate this immediately. We've got an intruder in the house. One of you call the police." Markus was already halfway across the kitchen when the cook stopped him.

"Sir, you don't understand. This is no intruder. It's not human."

A vision of Leichner in the library, saying the same thing, flashed into Markus's mind. For the first time, doubt crept in.

"What do you mean?" he asked.

"It's…it's a ghost. A demon. A thing, not of this world."

Markus stared at her for a few seconds. He had never been religious and didn't believe in all that mumbo-jumbo his mother had held so dear. Now he was expected to believe he had ghosts in his basement? He quashed the fear and strode out into the corridor. At the far end, the curtain that had been hung from floor to ceiling ruffled slightly in the merest of drafts.

A moment's hesitation and then Markus started toward it. He ignored the growing stench of death, reached the curtain and swept it aside.

Did he imagine the sigh? The stench grew impossible to ignore and he removed a clean handkerchief from his pocket. He clamped it to his nose and flicked the light switch. Amazing that the electricity still worked, even after all those years of disuse.

The illuminated bare room had been walled up for so long, anything could have died in here. A rat or mouse most probably. The wall had only come down earlier today and revealed nothing of interest except a small, square room with walls on three sides and a door. Heavy, locked and no key. The workmen would knock it down tomorrow.

Markus stepped inside. The floor was stone flagged and dusty. The walls were yellowing plaster, with a few hairline cracks but nothing significant. He bent down. Through the keyhole, he could barely make out another room. Against the far wall there seemed to be some furniture, but too indistinct to identify. Would this be where they found the Klimt?

He was about to step away when he caught a slight movement. He peered closer. Then jumped back as if he had been shot.

A black, red-veined eye met his. And he didn't imagine the raucous laugh that accompanied it.

Markus sped back across the room, tossed the curtain aside and dashed down the corridor. In the kitchen three pairs of scared eyes met his.

Still slumped in the chair, Frau Palfry spoke slowly. "You saw it too, didn't you?"

"I...I'm not sure. I thought I saw an eye. Through the keyhole. But that isn't possible.

Frau Palfry nodded. The others looked on. The cook still clutched her chest.

"She said the dead walk in this house." The housekeeper's voice was expressionless.

Markus fought to bring his breathing back to normal. "Who said that?"

"Magda Varga. She told my uncle, her brother Ferenc, just before she went missing. He tried to warn me about this house, but I ignored him. As the years went by and nothing happened, I forgot his words."

"Where is your uncle now? I must speak to him."

"In a cemetery. In Budapest. He died two years ago."

"What else do you know, Frau Palfry? Is there anyone I can speak to? Anyone who is still alive and remembers this house from before those rooms were walled up?"

Frau Palfry's lips were colorless, her skin almost transparent. The shock she had received mere minutes ago seemed to have aged her ten years.

"Maybe one person. She was a typist. My uncle said she was at the heart of everything that happened here. Maybe she is still alive. She will be old if she is. In her eighties."

"Do you have a name for this lady? I must find her."

"Her name is Adeline Ogilvy."

Chapter 17

Wimbledon, London

Adeline Ogilvy removed her reading glasses and set them down on the small table next to her chair. She picked up the letter in her lap and set it down beside them, before raising herself to her feet. These days, even a relatively short period of inactivity made her joints lock, and her first few steps were unsteady as she began her slow progress from her living room to the kitchen, where she filled the kettle and switched it on.

She had become a creature of habit these days. Up at eight thirty every morning, she would potter about doing light housework where dust had dared to land. Eleven o'clock would see her fix her hat firmly, with a hatpin, on her neatly permed white hair. Most days, she would don a coat—lightweight and showerproof for summer, warm tweed for winter and the colder days of spring and autumn. On her feet, serviceable well-fitting shoes. Painful bunions meant that comfort had long been preferable over fashion. Then, with her handbag over her arm and her wicker shopping basket in hand, she would open the door of her little terraced house and start her slow walk to the local shops.

Adeline would occasionally enter one of the new supermarkets but preferred the personal service of the greengrocer she had known since he was a baby and the baker whose bread warmed and comforted her with its fresh baked, homey smell wafting from his shop into the street.

That particular morning, Adeline had decided against negotiating a too-narrow aisle with a trolley whose wheels wanted to move in separate directions. More than once, this had resulted in her pushing harder and harder, only to need rescuing from a teetering stack of baked beans by a spotty fifteen-year-old male assistant. No, today, she would exchange pleasantries with obliging shopkeepers in their own small establishments.

The streets of Wimbledon were far busier these days and the street noise had changed. She rarely saw a horse and cart —with the exception of the occasional brewer's dray and the rag and bone man. She frowned at the stench of oil, diesel, and petrol, as the cars whizzed by and motorbikes careered past. They seemed especially keen to make as much noise as possible, revving up as they passed her. She was remembering the old days of horses clip-clopping along, leaving piles of steaming manure behind them. A wry smile creased the corners of her lips. Perhaps not such good old days after all.

At that moment, the dreadful teenager from across the street whizzed past in his battered and rusting Ford Anglia; its multi-tone horn competing with the blaring car radio.

"Is that really necessary?" Adeline realized she had voiced her displeasure out loud, much to the amusement of a young man in a suit, who tipped his hat to her.

"There's talk of banning those things," he said, smiling.

"What? Teenagers in souped-up cars?"

He laughed. "No, those car horns."

"Well, all I can say is, it can't come soon enough."

The man smiled again and went on his way. Adeline continued up to the shops as she did every day except Sunday. Her Sunday routine largely depended on the weather. If fine, she might venture into the park and walk along the paths, admiring the trees, shrubs, and flowers, except in late autumn and winter of course. Then she tended to hibernate in front of her cheery fire, read a book or maybe watch an old film on television. Sometimes she might listen to a play on the radio, or even potter about in her tiny back garden.

At eighty-four, Adeline knew she must remain as active as she possibly could. The minute she gave way to the aches and pains of rheumatism and sheer old age, the sooner her joints would atrophy, and that was unthinkable.

The kettle boiled and Adeline warmed her teapot with a little of the boiling water, emptied it, added two spoons of tea leaves and boiled the kettle again.

Never make tea with water that has been allowed to go off the boil.

Her mother reckoned she could always tell if someone had done that.

"The tea has no flavor," she used to say.

Adeline had found no reason to doubt her.

Five minutes later, Adeline brought her tea tray into the living room and moved her reading glasses and letter before setting it down on the table. She poured her tea and eased herself back down into her chair.

She took a couple of sips of the scalding drink and set her cup and saucer down on the tray. Adeline retrieved her glasses and reread the unexpected letter.

> *My dear Mrs. Ogilvy,*
>
> *I trust you will forgive the intrusion, but I find I am in urgent need of your help.*
>
> *I am the present owner of a house in Hietzing, Vienna, in which I understand you used to live and work for some weeks during 1913, at which time, I am given to understand, some extraordinary events took place. I believe you knew a woman by the name of Magda Varga who was the aunt of my housekeeper. She related these events to her brother, Ferenc—my housekeeper's uncle. Sadly, soon after she did so, Magda Varga disappeared and no trace has ever been found of her.*

Adeline raised her head and tears welled up in her eyes. How many times had she thought of dear, brave Magda over the years? She had imagined her married, with children, all grown up and with children of their own no doubt. But all the time, Magda hadn't been living any sort of life. From this letter, it sounded as if everyone believed she was dead. That house… that evil place. Did Quintillus have a hand in her disappearance?

She went back to her reading.

> *My reason for contacting you is to tell you that, after years of peace, something is once again happening in my home. It seems to center on the basement and particularly around an area which was walled up long ago, but which I, in my foolishness, sought to open up in my quest for a long-lost painting. I believe you may have been familiar with it. The artist was Gustav Klimt and the portrait is a representation of Cleopatra.*

At the second reading, the impact of what was happening in that house hit her much harder than the first time. Not that the writer had gone into any great detail, but his description of the figure he had seen, brought memories of Quintillus's hideous form flooding into Adeline's brain.

She read on to the end, careful not to miss a single word, looking for a mention of the gold statuette of Set, but there was none. That, at least, was a blessing.

She read the signature "Markus von Dürnstein." The letter was headed with his family crest and the paper was the finest quality. His handwriting was almost copperplate and his English impeccable. His name was vaguely familiar, and Adeline had a dim memory of a newspaper article she had read in *The Sunday Times* recently. Count Markus von Dürnstein pictured with the Prime Minister, Harold Wilson. Some trade deal. Adeline remembered it only because of the contrast between the two men. Harold Wilson wore his trademark Gannex overcoat with his pipe in his hand. The count stood a few inches taller, smartly dressed in a dark suit. The photograph showing the two men shaking hands was posed and false. The count's smile seemed pasted on for the camera.

This influential man had sought her out. He was offering to come to London or to pay her flight out to Vienna. If she took the latter option, she was welcome to stay as his guest. Adeline shuddered. On no account could she stay in that house. She didn't even want to enter that place. She remembered how insistent Professor Mayer had been that she never return under any circumstances. Adeline could hardly believe herself. She was actually considering taking the count up on his offer. Up to a point. She would have to stay somewhere, and, on her restricted income, she couldn't afford to pay for it herself. No matter. The count had anticipated that option as well. He was offering to pay for her accommodation in a luxury hotel.

He had included his telephone number and asked her to call him, reversing the charges.

Adeline's mind wandered back over the years and an image of Gustav Klimt flashed into her mind. The way she had felt in his presence. No man had ever had that effect on her since. How many times she had wished she had taken him up on his offer and posed for him. She could have made it work. She could have gone to his studio at weekends. Would she have become his mistress? She sighed.

But a sudden memory of Quintillus soured her reverie, stained her mood, and drove all pleasant thoughts out of her mind. Her rational self knew that dead or not, he would have found a way to ruin it. He destroyed everything and everyone with whom he came into contact. Nothing would have stopped him from pursuing his obsession to make Cleopatra his own.

Adeline struggled to her feet once more and limped at first as she made her way into the hall. The lone telephone in the house rested on a London directory on top of a purpose-built table, which incorporated a padded seat. She lowered herself onto it with a little difficulty. She would have to add a couple of cushions to it before long. It really was a bit low for her these days.

She touched the phone, hesitated, removed her hand and weighed up her options. She could, of course, ignore the count's request. Part of her mind screamed at her to do just that. She could carry on her comfortable life here, with all its habits and routines, or she could put herself in danger again. Because whatever other option she chose would lead inevitably in that direction.

Markus von Dürnstein could come to London. That posed far fewer risks for Adeline. She had almost convinced herself that this is what she would propose. He could come here, they could discuss what was going on and then… What? He would go away again, knowing a little more, but still unable to do anything.

Adeline forced herself to admit something she had suppressed for over fifty years. Those terrifying weeks in Vienna had left an indelible impression on her. For weeks, months, even years afterward, she would wake screaming in the night. She would see Emeryk Quintillus's mummified skin and eyeless face.

When was the last time she had dreamed of it?

Last week.

There was unfinished business in Vienna, and she wouldn't resolve it by staying here.

Adeline made her decision, took a ragged breath, and picked up the receiver.

Chapter 18

Entering Café Central, Markus scanned the shabby room for the person he was about to meet for the first time. He could hardly miss her. She seemed so out of time and like her photograph. She was dressed in a tweed tailored jacket, her snow-white hair newly permed. Her smart brown hat, with its old-fashioned hatpin, completed the look of an elderly British lady.

She didn't register him immediately. When she did, she gave a little start.

"Oh, do please forgive me." Her German was pleasantly accented. "I was miles away then. I was remembering Dr. Trotsky. He used to play chess with Viktor Adler over there." She pointed to a nearby table. "And once, I'm sure I saw Sigmund Freud eating chocolate cake." She glanced around at the walls, nicotine stained from many years of heavy smokers and neglect. "Of course, much like the rest of us, this place has seen better days. Still, nothing a strong will and a few million schillings couldn't put right." Her eyes sparkled and she smiled—the whole effect taking at least forty years off her age

Markus returned the smile and spoke in English. "May I introduce myself? I am Markus von Dürnstein." He extended his hand.

The woman took it, her smart kid glove soft against his palm. "And I thought I would never return to Vienna, but, as I said on the telephone, your letter meant I had to come. I am Adeline Ogilvy and I believe we have much to discuss."

Markus sat down opposite her and smiled as his guest slipped back into near-flawless German to order a mélange and a slice of chocolate cake.

"Do you speak German in England?" he asked.

"I haven't spoken a word since I left Vienna in 1913," she replied. "But I've ordered what I always had when I came here. It all came back to me."

"I am happy to speak English. I always need to practice. I have many business interests in your country."

"Yes, I saw you in *The Sunday Times* with our Prime Minister. From your expression, I got the impression you weren't very keen on him."

Markus waved his hand in a dismissive gesture. "We are from two different worlds, I think. And I found his accent a little hard to understand. He insisted on smoking that pipe and the tobacco smelled so dreadful my eyes watered. By the time the photographers were allowed to take their pictures, my eyes were stinging and the room was a fog of smoke."

Adeline smiled and sipped the coffee that had been placed in front of her.

"That would explain the forced smile."

Markus laughed and stirred his espresso.

Adeline took a bite of the light cake and Markus a forkful of crumbly apple strudel.

His companion swallowed and touched her napkin to her lips. "Would you like to tell me exactly what has been going on in your home?"

Markus laid his fork down. He took a deep breath and recounted every detail he could recall about the horrors of his basement.

Adeline listened. Her mélange grew cold and was replaced by a hot one. When the count had finished, she took a gulp of coffee, perhaps in the hope its strength would fortify her.

"How is the staff managing?"

"They are… managing. All except the new girl. She left on the day my housekeeper was attacked. I have managed to erect some boarding, from floor to ceiling, in the hope that will keep whatever it is locked in, but something bangs on it from the other side. So I have instructed my staff to go nowhere near that corridor. The wine cellar is out of bounds and the door to the corridor is kept firmly shut and locked. They don't talk much about it to me, but I feel we are all waiting for something to happen."

"You could simply leave. You do have other properties, don't you?"

"Yes, but not in Vienna. I have thought of moving to a hotel until this is all resolved, but I am scared of what it will do if left unchecked. That house has been in my family for over forty years. There are valuable, irreplaceable Klimt paintings. If the house is left empty, thieves might break in and vandalize them…" Markus's voice faltered. Now he had spoken the words and seen the bemused expression on Adeline's face, he felt foolish. These were mere possessions.

Adeline cleared her throat as if trying to remove a stubborn obstruction. "My dear count, Emeryk Quintillus is evil. He is not a person you can lock up in the normal sense of the word. If the house has been quiet all these years, and the basement rooms I remember have been walled up, then supernatural forces have been at work to contain his evil. I don't know what those might be, but you have definitely unleashed him through breaking down that wall. I doubt very much that any frail wooden board is going to be strong enough to contain him. I think you know that anyway. In your place, I would shut the house up, buy another one and take your loyal staff with you."

"And leave that evil roaming free? Supposing it latches onto someone else?"

"I don't think it can. Not unless they are related to Cleopatra."

Markus dropped his fork with a clatter on the plate. Several people turned to see what had happened, then looked back again. "Did you say, 'related to Cleopatra'? My aunt, by marriage, was supposedly related to Cleopatra. She was the one I told you about who went missing along with her husband. My uncle."

"Interesting. I am also related to Cleopatra. At least that's what Professor Lansdowne at Oxford University said many years ago. That's why I was chosen for Quintillus's assignment. It's what brought me to Vienna."

"But you are not, as far as you are aware, related to Irina Feodorovna Ivanova, formerly of St. Petersburg?"

"Not that I'm aware of, but I suppose I might be, somewhere along the line." Adeline told Markus what Professor Mayer had said regarding why she had been chosen for the job. She also told him about the curious business of Quintillus's lawyers who seemed to have disappeared and were never traced, despite Miss Sinclair's best efforts. She had given up in the end, considerably out of pocket.

"You told me, on the telephone, that the professor instructed you never to return to the house and not even to Vienna. I understand the house, but why the entire city?"

Adeline shook her head. "I've never been sure about that. Maybe he feared that if I was in the same city as Quintillus's restless spirit, it would somehow sense my presence…"

She stopped, raised her napkin to cover her mouth, and stared at Markus, who reached forward and touched her hand.

"Forgive me for stating the obvious," he said. "But here you are."

"I should never have come back here."

"But here you are. And we have no choice. We must deal with this. Together."

Adeline lowered the napkin. "The servants must leave that house. Can they go and stay in your house in Styria, where your butler is? You shouldn't stay in that house, either. Not until we know what we are dealing with."

Markus considered this for a few moments. It made sense. The servants could do with a well-earned rest after their recent ordeals. If he and Adeline were there every day, it wouldn't seem as if the place was empty.

"Very well. I will make the necessary arrangements this afternoon. Styria is very beautiful in late spring." He smiled.

"Can you arrange for builders to replace that wall?"

"Ah, that is more difficult. I'm afraid word spreads fast. So far, no builder within a ten-kilometer radius of Vienna is willing to take on the job. They're keen enough at first but when my housekeeper gives them the address, they suddenly have a big job on and cannot possibly do it for at least six months, probably a year. Maybe more."

"Keep trying. Although, by now, it's probably too late anyway. Thank goodness you didn't break the door down into the room where the portrait was. At least you don't have the statue. *That* was lost in the train wreck near Trieste. When I received your letter, I was worried it might have resurfaced, but... What's the matter? Oh no, don't tell me..."

Markus nodded slowly. "My uncle—Irina's husband—found it lying on the rail track. He knew Irina loved Egyptian artifacts, so he gave it to her. It disappeared the same day they did. I've always assumed my uncle took it down to the basement, to stand with the portrait."

"The very worst thing he could have done. That would have sealed their fate for sure. The statue, reunited with Cleopatra's mummy's dust which Gustav Klimt unwittingly painted into the picture. This is what Quintillus wanted all along. It was in his plans for me. I was supposed to be the reincarnation of his beloved ancient queen, but I escaped his clutches. Then fate brought Irina to him."

"And this time he succeeded."

"Thanks to the combined power of the statuette and the dust."

"But they were walled up. Who would do that?"

"Someone who hated one or both of them very much indeed and who had the ear of a powerful god." Adeline told Markus about Arsinoe.

When she finished, Markus leaned back, his brain awash with impossible thoughts. "If what you're saying is true, we need to separate the picture and the statuette."

"The professor believed it imperative to return the statuette to the mummy of the real Cleopatra at Taposiris Magna. We were on our way there when the train crashed. I was told Serbian nationalists were responsible for blowing it up, but I have always thought it strange that just before the explosion, I saw a strange glow in the sky, like the one I used to see in your house. I have long come to the conclusion that, where Quintillus is concerned, there are no coincidences."

"He caused the train wreck?"

"Yes, or some power related to this did. Maybe it was Arsinoe, although I can't think why. It surely couldn't be Cleopatra, so who does that leave?"

"That god. Set?"

"Maybe, but only if his power was invoked somehow. That statuette was very powerful, but there would have to be a reason."

Markus stroked his chin. "Such as Quintillus wanting to ensure it returned to him, and because my uncle found it, that wish was always going to be granted. Its power led to him and Irina choosing to buy that house, with its strange resident housekeeper."

"Yes, curious that she should be living there." Adeline folded her napkin. "Did you know her name?"

"My uncle did tell me." He searched his mind for the name. "Josefa someone."

Adeline's eyes shot open. "Lederer?"

"Yes. Did you know her?"

"You might say that. She was the cook in Quintillus's day. The last time I saw her body, it was being loaded onto a cart and she was most assuredly dead. Magda shot her. And then Ferenc and Istvan drove her away, only to report she had disappeared a day later."

"I suppose we can finally guess what happened to Magda."

Adeline nodded. "It wouldn't take a genius to picture Josefa—or rather, Arsinoe—wreaking her revenge."

A little while later, Markus paid the bill and offered to hail a cab to take them the short distance to the Hotel Sacher where Adeline had already checked in and Markus had now decided to stay.

"Let's walk, shall we?" Adeline said. "It's such good exercise. I try to get out as much as possible, especially when the weather is like this."

They stepped out in the spring sunshine. Adeline looked around and smiled. "Despite two world wars and the terrible Allied bombing raids in 1945, not a lot changes in this city."

"So much had to be rebuilt. The opera house, the cathedral. There is still much to do."

"I know. I saw that film. *The Third Man*. But the restoration is remarkably close to the original."

Markus nodded. He walked beside her, taking care not to hurry her. For a lady of eighty-four, she was remarkably fit and walked without a stick, but he imagined her pace had been considerably quicker when she was first here.

The smartly uniformed staff of the Hotel Sacher treated Markus with great deference. They all knew who he was and of his reputation for providing generous gratuities. Adeline made her way up to her room to relax in the luxurious surroundings. Markus headed for the bar. He needed a stiff drink.

The house was deathly quiet. Adeline looked around, a feeling of trepidation building inside her. The hall was much lighter than it had been. White walls gave it a clean, almost clinical feel. The marble floor looked new. Even the old, heavy door to the kitchen and basement had been replaced with one that matched the others leading off into the various rooms. Only the staircase seemed to have been untouched by renovation.

Markus led the way into the library and Adeline caught her breath at the vivid ceiling.

"Of course, you will remember it before it deteriorated," he said. "Perhaps you will be so kind as to tell me whether the restorers have done a good job?"

Adeline took in the exquisite detail of Cleopatra, her handmaidens and the historic scene. She nodded. "From memory, I would say they have done a job of which the artist would have been proud. This is precisely as I remember it."

Markus smiled. "Good. I'm afraid I spent a fortune, but I love this ceiling, so to hear that makes it worth the expense. I can stop having a guilty conscience."

"Most assuredly." Adeline took in the rest of the library. The spiral staircase was still there, and the books seemed unchanged from Quintillus's day.

"I developed quite a taste for the works of H.G. Wells while I stayed here," she said. "Do you still have them? Dr. Quintillus had amassed quite a collection."

"I should imagine so. I'm no great reader myself, I'm afraid. Neither were either of my uncles who owned this house before me. I should think you would still find the books you read and probably in the place you last put them too."

Adeline had moved toward the window and peered at the wood paneled wall to the right of it.

"Where's the door?" she asked.

Markus raised his eyebrows. "Door?"

Adeline pointed. "There used to be a door there. Quite a small, narrow one. It led down to the basement. There's another one hidden in the wall of the doctor's bedroom. They led directly down to corridors which take you to the rooms I told you about."

"I'm sorry, I don't know about any such thing."

Adeline sighed. She peered closer at the wall. No sign there had ever been an entrance there.

"Shall we go up? I would like to check in Dr. Quintillus's room. Oh, I'm sorry. It's your room now."

"No matter. Please. Show me the room you mean."

Adeline took one step at a time and remembered how she had dashed up and down this staircase many a time in the fraught weeks she had lived here. Creaky knee joints and a tricky hip weren't going to allow such progress this time. Finally, slightly breathless, she made it to the top and turned down the corridor, which was no longer dark, but also sported white walls. This owner had a much more modern taste.

She arrived at the door she needed and hesitated.

"Allow me." Markus turned the handle. Adeline's palms broke into a cold sweat. Inside the room, nothing appeared to remain of its earlier owner. A modern double divan bed had been made up with a bright floral cover and matching curtains. The fireplace was purely decorative, with a large vase of dried flowers in the hearth. A lilac deep-pile fitted carpet caressed her feet and Adeline noticed that Markus had removed his shoes. She did likewise. When she moved, it felt like walking on a soft cloud.

The wall behind the bed had also been decorated in pale lilac. No sign of the hidden entrance. Adeline moved closer and ran her hands along the surface, failing to find any trace of that entrance she and the Professor had used so many years before.

"Somebody did a marvelous job of sealing this wall," she said.

"That's another part of the mystery of this house," Markus said. "The architect has conducted all sorts of tests on the walls. He looked particularly for secret entrances such as the ones you've described, but he found nothing, except in the basement when he found the hollow space behind that wall."

"Do you use this room at all? It's very lovely."

"My nieces use it when they come to visit me. I have three, all in their twenties. My sister's daughters. I love them with all my heart, but I'm very glad they don't all descend on me at once. One is getting married next year, so I suppose I won't see so much of her after that."

"I never had children myself," Adeline said. "But your nieces must be a blessing to you." Adeline suppressed the rush of emotion that always went with any mention of offspring, or family of any kind.

If she had ever been able to get over those weeks in Vienna maybe she would have found someone else. Someone she could marry and live a normal life with. But the First World War had come along, decimating an entire generation of young men. She was older than most of the young women who never found anyone to marry them, and no one ever wandered into her sphere. Her cherished memories of her late husband were all she had to keep her warm at night.

Adeline carried the burden of everything that had happened to her; a constant feeling that she was, in some way, a freak. How could she ever explain to a future husband all she and the professor had been through? And she could never keep such a thing secret. Besides, the screaming nightmares would warrant an explanation alone.

Then World War Two came along and, instead of retiring, she threw herself into war work, using her typing and office skills in a variety of worthwhile roles. At the end of the war, she found herself consigned to the life of a pensioner. The past seemed so far away. Now it had returned.

Adeline was filled with a sudden desire to escape the sunny room.

"I think perhaps we should go down to the basement," she said, surprising herself with how steady her voice was. She replaced her shoes.

Markus led the way.

The kitchen felt cold. No one around.

"The cook left for Styria this morning," Markus said. "My housekeeper has gone to stay with her sister in Linz, and my butler is still away. We are completely alone in this house."

"I doubt that," Adeline said. A sudden chill blew across the back of her neck.

"Did you feel that?" she asked.

Markus nodded.

Adeline hugged herself. "Now do you think we are alone in this house?"

He shook his head. He took down a small, but vicious-looking, meat cleaver from a rack on the wall. Inside his jacket was a deep pocket, which occasionally held a revolver. Mercifully, the handle of the cleaver slid in and his lapel concealed the blade. He buttoned the jacket. "I don't know why I'm doing this, but it helps."

Adeline understood. The forces of evil might not succumb to a blow from a sharp blade, but at least the person carrying it could feel they were protected from anything of human origin.

Markus led her past the wine cellar. In front of them, a large board sealed the entrance to the newly rediscovered room. They both slowed down; each seeming not to want to disturb anything that might be listening on the other side.

Markus put his finger to his lips and placed his ear against the board. Silence.

Seconds ticked by and became a minute, then two.

A long, low groan echoed down the corridor. Adeline grabbed Markus's arm.

"It's starting," she whispered.

Something hit the board with the force of a charging bull. Markus fell back. He scrambled to his feet.

Another crash. Another. The board shook but held firm. Sawdust showered down from the edges, coating the floor.

A green light began to pulse and glow, only the narrowest of shards visible at the edges of the board.

Markus leaned close to Adeline, who still clung to his arm, her knuckles white, the skin stretched taut across them. "I can't imagine how, but I think it knows you're here."

Adeline nodded. He might think it. She was certain of it.

Markus cleared his throat. Surely he wasn't going to talk to it? She shook her head violently, in a vain attempt to stop him. He ignored her.

"Dr. Quintillus. My name is Markus von Dürnstein and you are in my house."

Another crash and the board bowed in the middle before righting itself. It really couldn't take much more of that. Adeline clung tighter to Markus.

"Dr. Quintillus," Markus began again. "I realize you feel aggrieved by all that has happened, but you must leave my house. You are done here. You cannot remain trapped in there forever."

A cold, raucous laugh filled Adeline with dread.

Markus let out a cry. "My God, it's not coming from in there. It's out here, with us."

Adeline's eyes grew wide as she stared down the corridor. She pointed a shaking hand. "That's him!"

Emeryk Quintillus's skin was fresh and pink. He looked human…but when he came within a few feet of them and stopped, the death in his eyes chilled Adeline. He had no soul, his body an empty shell of evil.

She inhaled deeply. She must not show any of the fear or panic that gripped her spine. Markus placed his arm protectively around her shoulders, but Adeline stood firm.

Quintillus pointed at Adeline. "She is mine."

Markus coughed. "What do you want with an old lady?"

Quintillus's stare was difficult to bear, but Adeline concentrated on breathing steadily and maintaining eye contact.

When he spoke, his voice cracked—as dry as he himself had been last time Adeline had seen him. "She is not old," he said. "She is mine."

"She is most assuredly *not* yours," Markus said. "Now, leave my house. You are done here."

Quintillus raised his arm, as if about to strike him, but instead he opened his mouth to reveal rotten, blackened teeth. The stench of death poured out of him and a wheezing, as if a hundred trapped souls gasped their last breath, issued from his mouth.

A swirl of smoke coated the board in a veil of black. Markus pulled Adeline to one side. The wood cracked, broke, and cascaded to the floor in a cloud of dust. When Adeline dared to look, Quintillus had gone, and they stood on the threshold of the room she saw so often in her nightmares. The sickly stench of decay and decomposition hung heavily in the atmosphere.

The familiar hieroglyphics sprawled across one wall. The electric light was switched on, and two piles of clothes lay on the floor.

Markus held Adeline's hand and the two made their way in.

Markus pointed at the hieroglyphics. In a barely audible voice, he said, "I swear those weren't here before."

Adeline reached up to whisper to him. "We must look for the statuette. We have to get it away from here."

Her toe caught the edge of one of the piles of clothes and she clapped her hand over her mouth.

A mostly skeletal hand—its fingers outstretched—lay next to her foot. Diamonds gleamed in gold rings. A bony wrist wore an emerald and ruby bracelet. Shreds of decayed and mottled flesh still clung to the bones and the nails of the hand were torn—right off in some cases. Adeline swallowed bile.

The corpse's dress had once been sumptuous, but was now dusty, torn and speckled with dried reddish-brown blood.

Markus pulled her away.

Adeline allowed herself to be led. "Your aunt?" she whispered.

Markus nodded. "I believe so. And over there, if I am not mistaken is my uncle. But I don't understand how they can be here. They weren't before. Not when the builders first took down the wall."

Markus led her past Wilhelm's body, but not so quickly that she didn't see he was lying on his back, his face mostly eaten away by maggots and whatever other insect life had chosen to feed on him. Adeline wondered fleetingly if the scarabs had made a return visit.

The corpse's jawbone was visible and unhinged, twisted at an unnatural angle. Quintillus's handiwork no doubt. A huge black spider emerged from the dead count's ruined mouth. It scurried across the floor, into a dark corner.

"Adeline, look at the door. The scratches. How could I not have seen those before?"

Adeline tore her sickened gaze away from Markus's murdered relation and saw the gouges that had left deep tracks and ragged edges in the wood. "You didn't see them because you weren't meant to," she said. "Not then. Quintillus can create illusions. In your case you didn't see something that was there. In mine, I saw something that didn't happen." She gave a shudder as she remembered back over the years. Quintillus's head turning toward her, when the professor had seen no movement at all.

"My aunt must have tried to claw her way out." His voice was heavy with sadness.

"Hence the nails," Adeline swallowed the sourness in her mouth. "What a terrible way to die. Walled up in here with Quintillus."

Markus was staring at something on the wall, and, with a heavy heart, Adeline knew what it must be. What she had dreaded.

The portrait of Cleopatra. Once again on the wall, in profile.

Markus reached up.

"No, don't!"

"Oh, by all means, do so."

Quintillus stood at the entrance. He strode in. "I shall need that again. And the statue."

"But you took your Cleopatra," Markus pointed at the corpse of his aunt. "Surely her spirit is still with you."

Quintillus's lips curled in a grimace. "That body was mortal. It died. She was supposed to be mine for all eternity but once more, my beloved queen's spirit is trapped." He nodded toward the portrait. "I will set her free again."

"No," Adeline said, her voice strong and steady. "You will not do this again. Is it not enough that you have destroyed the lives of two people who lie dead in this room? Cleopatra doesn't want you. She would do anything to get away from you. She tried to claw her way out of here, she hated you so much. Maybe Irina, too, if anything of her remained in that body." Adeline pointed at the dead woman. "You can never have Cleopatra. She belongs to one man and that is the man she is buried with in Taposiris Magna."

"Adeline!" Markus grabbed her arms. "Don't antagonize him. You can see what he's capable of."

"No, Markus. Not him. The god. Set. I can see it all now. Set did this and he can do it again." She jabbed her finger at Quintillus. "You can do nothing without invoking the god's power."

Quintillus let out his raucous laugh. "You know nothing about me. Nothing. You are her descendant, as this woman was." He pointed at Irina. "My ancestor was Julius Caesar. Cleopatra would have been married to him if he had lived. I have always known my destiny. She never loved Mark Antony. He was expedient for her. Her spirit lives on. In that painting." He jabbed his finger at it. "It rejuvenates and restores itself. It is indestructible. All it needs is a vessel. A descendant to make it live. You will make it live. You will be eternally young and beautiful again—"

Adeline clenched her fists. "No, Quintillus. You tried once with me and failed. You will not succeed now. I'll kill myself first."

Quintillus took a step forward. Markus brandished the meat cleaver and sliced it through the air. The archeologist's right hand twitched on the floor. Blood gushed from the wound. A green radiance began to pulse from his jacket pocket.

Adeline wiped her mouth with the back of her hand. "Get the statue!"

Markus hesitated an instant, clearly shocked by what he'd done. It was a moment too long.

Quintillus lashed out with his stump, spraying blood over Markus. He chanted something in that ancient language Adeline hadn't heard for decades. She braced herself.

Markus was caught off balance and the cleaver clattered to the floor. It glowed red hot. Its blood spatters sizzled. Boiled. Evaporated.

The green light grew brighter, the pulsing more urgent with every second.

With a cry, Quintillus thrust his stump down onto the blade. He screamed. The smell of burning meat filled the air. Steam and smoke rose from the cleaver as the wound cauterized. Quintillus straightened himself and his eyes bored through Adeline's brain. She felt a tugging sensation, as if he was trying to wrench her soul from her body, to leave her as empty as he was. That was what he wanted. To drain her own soul and fill her body with Cleopatra's spirit. Out of the corner of her eye, Adeline saw the portrait twitch.

With a speed born of sheer desperation, she darted forward and grabbed the statuette from Quintillus's pocket. She brandished it high, feeling its power surging within her.

"You are finished, Quintillus," she said. "Now it is your turn to be cast out into oblivion."

Quintillus lunged forward but Markus was too quick. He sent the crazed doctor staggering, clutching his injured, and still smoking, arm.

On the far wall, a shadow formed into the jackal-headed god Adeline had hoped never to see again.

While she still held the statuette that bore his name, the god raised his staff. Quintillus seemed to sense what was coming. He cowered.

"No, it is my right. She is my queen."

A roar like a pride of lions filled the room. Quintillus screamed. A small army of scarabs poured down the walls, scurried across the floor and crawled up his body, their jaws snapping. They bit and left shriveled flesh. Rivulets of blood became gushing streams. The flesh peeled away, consumed by hundreds of ravenous, tiny mouths. Then they found his eyes, devouring the corneas, pupils, irises, until there was nothing left but bloody sockets. And all the while, Quintillus screamed until the insatiable insects chewed through his neck and consumed his larynx.

It took a mere couple of minutes before a fleshless skeleton collapsed onto the stone floor, its clothes in tatters.

Adeline lowered her arm. The statuette lay cold in her hand. Markus put his arm around her as the scarabs disintegrated into dust.

A small tornado smashed up the crackling, clattering bones, until a pile of grayish-white powder was all that was left of Dr. Emeryk Quintillus. It mingled with the remains of the scarabs. The shadow that had been Set dissolved.

Only the portrait remained.

Markus squeezed Adeline's arm. "Come, we still have work to do."

They left the house without a backward glance.

Chapter 19

Taposiris Magna

The helicopter landed on the site of the great temple of Taposiris Magna, sending clouds of sand and dust high into the air. As the blades slowed to a halt, Adeline and Markus waited for the air to clear before climbing down onto the stone ground. Markus held both of Adeline's hands as she stepped down from her first-ever helicopter ride.

"Thank you," she said, dusting off her cool cotton dress and adjusting her wide-brimmed hat.

Markus looked around him. The sky was a vivid, cloudless blue and despite the early hour—seven thirty a.m.—the heat already matched a fine summer afternoon in Vienna.

"Which way, I wonder." Markus surveyed the tall stone pylons and extensive ruins.

"I don't know, but the professor seemed to think that we would somehow be guided. By the statue I suppose."

In the helicopter, the pilot opened his newspaper and began to read.

Markus retrieved the statue from the pocket of his trousers and turned it over in his hand.

"Do you feel a compulsion to move in any particular direction?" Adeline asked.

Markus shook his head. He looked up and squinted at the far wall of the temple. "It looks more promising over there, though. I think some excavations may have been taking place."

Adeline fanned her face with her hat, before returning it to her head. She followed Markus. They crossed the few yards to a jumble of stones and debris.

Markus set the statuette on a partially raised stone slab and stepped back. Adeline stood next to him.

They waited. The only sound came from a slight breeze whistling through the ruins.

Minutes ticked by.

"I think we're in the wrong place." Markus made to retrieve the statuette. He stopped.

Beneath their feet, the earth rumbled.

"Earthquake?" Adeline felt the color drain from her face.

Markus shook his head. "I don't think so. But I do think we should move back."

He grabbed Adeline's hand and half-dragged her back toward the helicopter.

The rumbling grew louder, the ground shook; a pressure cooker of force built up underground. Suddenly, the stone slab shot up high into the air. It crashed down. Smashed into a thousand shards. Stone grated on stone. Sand swirled up into a cloud that set Markus and Adeline choking and covering their mouths and noses with their hands. Behind them, the Egyptian helicopter pilot had started the engine. The rotor blades began to turn.

He called out to them. "Come now. You must come *at once*. You don't see what I see. Come now!"

He lifted Adeline into the helicopter and reached for Markus. Adeline coughed. Her eyes streamed. She dabbed at them with a handkerchief and stared across at the dust storm that had taken on a green phosphorescence.

Beside her, Markus choked on dust.

"Did *we* do it?" Adeline asked him.

The helicopter took off and gave a swerve that sent Adeline's stomach sinking. Markus finally managed to speak

"I believe so." Markus called to the pilot. "Could you circle around here for a few minutes, until the dust settles? We want to fly over that site."

The pilot shot them a horrified look. "But, sir, it is not safe. Look to your right. There is something there."

Adeline and Markus saw the sight that had so frightened the pilot. Rising above the cloud of dust and sand, a huge figure with a jackal's head brandished a staff. Adeline caught her breath.

"Set," she said. "He has come to claim his image and return it to its rightful place."

Markus exhaled. "Then we have succeeded."

"I hope so. Yes, surely we have." If Adeline could convince herself that it was finally over, she might at last be able to sleep soundly after all these years.

"Sir." The pilot was pleading now.

"You have enough fuel to fly over the site, correct?" Markus asked.

"Yes, sir, but—"

"I'll triple your fee if you do it. Agreed?"

The pilot hesitated. When he spoke, he sounded subdued, nervous even. But Adeline knew he had been offered more money than he could expect to earn in a month. She had been with them when Markus agreed the higher-than-average fee, designed to buy his silence, along with his flying skills.

The pilot hesitated, but only for a few seconds. "Yes, sir. Agreed."

The sight that greeted them when the sandstorm died down and they flew directly overhead was extraordinary. A long, steep flight of stone steps led down between two high walls. At the foot, the emerald glow pulsed brightly.

"It is the work of the devil," the pilot said. The fingers of his right hand worked furiously at the bright blue worry beads he clutched.

"Circle around once more," Markus said.

The pilot muttered something in Arabic but did as he was bid.

This time, the glow faded. The noise of the helicopter drowned out whatever grating noise emanated from below. The stone walls closed in and concealed Cleopatra's tomb once more.

"Back to Alexandria," Markus called to the pilot who didn't need telling twice, by the stomach-churning speed at which he turned the helicopter.

"What will you do now?" Adeline asked. "Return to Vienna and live in that house?"

Markus shook his head. "Certainly not yet. Maybe never. I don't think I can ever feel safe in it after what's happened. I'll import some unsuspecting builder from Turkey, put him up in the house and get him to build the wall before he hears any of the rumors. Then maybe I'll sell it, but only to someone who can prove they're not descended from Cleopatra."

Adeline smiled.

Markus looked at her hard. She flinched under his gaze. So intense. Like he was trying to see inside her head.

"What will you do, Adeline? Back to your little house in Wimbledon?"

"It suits me well enough. I have my memories. And now this is resolved, I can put the bad ones firmly in a drawer, knowing Quintillus no longer controls any part of my life."

"I would like to invite you to my niece's wedding, as my personal guest. After all we've been through together, you feel like part of my family. And, I suppose your possible relationship to my late aunt means you are."

Tears sprang to Adeline's eyes. She could think of nothing she would like more. To be part of this man's family. "That is so kind of you, Markus. I shall be delighted to accept."

"Then it is done. Consider yourself an honorary aunt of the von Dürnstein family."

Adeline smiled, squeezed Markus's hand and watched the sands of Egypt drift far below them.

———

In the basement of the Königsberg House, a breeze wafted through. It shifted dust and ashes and swirled around. It stopped. The dust and debris settled. A woman stood over it.

"And now, Doctor, you and I can make our peace. One day you will need me to help you. Only I can get you what you want."

The portrait shifted on the wall. A sigh echoed around the room.

The dust began to collect. Mesh together. Reform itself.

Arsinoe threw back her head and laughed.

Afterword

Lakeside Care Home, Wimbledon, London
August 1980

"My goodness. One hundred years old today. Cook's baking a birthday cake for you." The slender Jamaican Care Assistant smoothed Adeline's sheets and tucked her in securely.

Adeline liked the girl. Jennifer. Always had a smile on her face and exuded a pleasant aroma of oranges. Whether she ate a lot of them or wore some kind of orange essence Adeline didn't know, but it was a comforting, fresh smell. Such a welcome change from the all-too frequent mingling antiseptic aromas of disinfectant and bleach that tingled her nose and caught at the back of her throat. Still, even that was far better than…

Adeline settled herself back against her just-fluffed pillows. Jennifer could pummel a pillow into submission in seconds.

"Someone from the local paper is coming to take your photograph, while you hold the telegram from the Queen, and the other residents are all looking forward to your party."

"Will there be champagne?" Adeline asked. She winked at the Care Assistant. "It's not a celebration without champagne."

Jennifer laughed. "Oh, I don't know about that, but…" She tapped the side of her nose. "I'll see what I can do."

Adeline smiled. "You're a good girl, Jennifer. Even if you do try and scare me with these daft magazines of yours."

Jennifer laughed. "Oh, you know you like them really. Anyway, I wouldn't have started bringing them in if you hadn't told me about that haunted house in Vienna."

And if I'd told you the real story about that house, you wouldn't have found it so delicious.

"Oh, I nearly forgot," Jennifer said. "Talking about that, I've brought in the latest *Haunted House* magazine and I'm not sure if it's your house or not, but there's one in there. A haunted mansion in Vienna. Someone took a photograph and this weird apparition… Hang on, I'll go and get it for you. It's really scary."

Jennifer bustled out of the room.

Adeline heaved herself up into a sitting position. Arthritis, rheumatism, and now this damned osteoporosis made any movement painful and awkward. She winced. Dear Jennifer. Yet more photographic trickery no doubt. Of course, it wasn't beyond the bounds of possibility that it could be the same house. Poor, dear Markus had died three years earlier, and the house had fallen into disrepair long before that. He'd tried to sell it, but too many people knew of its shady history. Goodness alone knew what state those wonderful Klimt paintings were in now.

Jennifer returned. "Hey, you should have waited. Let me help you." She dropped the magazine on the bed and hurried to lift Adeline into a more comfortable position. She then sat down on a chair next to the bed and flicked through the pages until she found the article she wanted.

"Here we are." She handed it to Adeline.

"I'll need my glasses. The print's all blurry."

Jennifer handed them to her and she put them on. Instantly a recognizable house came into focus.

"The Horrifically Haunted Königsberg House of Vienna," she read. "Typical lurid headline." She smiled, but inside her an uncomfortable niggling feeling began. The more she read on, the more that unease grew.

The new owner of the Königsberg House in Vienna's exclusive Hietzing district had the fright of her life when she was photographing her home prior to renovation. Down in the basement of the mansion she found a derelict room. She photographed it and when the picture was developed, a shadowy figure was revealed. You can see it on page 77.

Jennifer touched her hand "Mrs. Ogilvy? Are you all right? You're trembling."

Adeline raised her eyes. She must keep calm. "I'm not sure, Jennifer. I seem to be all thumbs today. Please could you find page seventy-seven for me?

"Of course." Jennifer's look of concern wasn't lost on Adeline. "Here we are."

She returned the magazine, open at the right page. The black and white quarter page photograph was grainy. But in amongst the room's rubble and detritus, a familiar figure stood in one corner. Black, empty eye-sockets. On his head, a stovepipe hat.

The page swam in front of her. She dropped the magazine, her hands no longer able to hold it.

"Mrs. Ogilvy! Oh my God!" The sound of the emergency bell faded into the background as Adeline sank lower and lower into blackness.

Jennifer's lilting voice sidled into Adeline's sleep and roused her. Over the past three weeks since her stroke, she had found it hard to stay awake for more than a couple of hours.

The Care Assistant had someone with her. "Such a shame," she said. "Her stroke has left her pretty much paralyzed. She can't speak and she can only move her left arm. But she can see and hear and when you look into her eyes you know her mind's as alert as ever."

Another woman spoke, but Adeline couldn't make out the words. The stranger was speaking so quietly it barely registered as a whisper.

"Oh, I'm sure she'll be delighted to see you. She often mentioned the old days. Her memory was as sharp as a scalpel. I miss hearing her stories. Of course, I was never sure if she had made them all up."

If you only knew.

Jennifer's voice moved closer and Adeline opened her eyes. The smiling face with the brilliant white teeth came into focus, along with her familiar comforting scent.

"Ah, you're awake, Mrs. Ogilvy. I've brought someone to see you. She's come ever such a long way. You'll never believe it, but she lives in that house in the magazine you were reading. The one in Vienna…"

Adeline's eyes opened wider.

Jennifer's smile vanished, replaced in an instant by a quizzical expression. She stepped back, taking her scent of oranges with her. This time when she spoke, she sounded a little uncertain. "I'll… leave you two alone for a bit… Give you a chance to chat."

Adeline willed her mouth to open. *Don't leave me.* But only her mind screamed the words.

A heavy aroma enveloped her. One she had hoped never to smell again. Lilies.

A woman's face bent over her. Swam into focus. Olive skin. Black hair.

Violet eyes gazed down at her.

But that was impossible.

It couldn't be…

Adeline closed her eyes and prayed.

Acknowledgments

Many thanks to Julia Kavan, who gave me such good advice the first time around. Thanks also to all my writer friends — and a special shout-out to one we have lost since Wrath of the Ancients first appeared — Susan Roebuck, gone from us far too soon. Fly free, dear lady.

Thanks also to the staff at the Remise Transport Museum in Vienna for ensuring I put Adeline on the right tram in 1913. That was a fascinating morning!

Huge thanks to Crossroad Press who are always such a joy to work with. This story and its two sequels have found their true home.

And, if you are reading this, then many thanks to you. If you enjoyed this trip to Vienna, you really should go and visit the real thing. As they say in that most beautiful and enigmatic of cities — *Wien ist anders* (Vienna is different).

Viel Spaß!

About the Author

Following a varied career in sales, advertising and career guidance, Catherine Cavendish is now the full-time author of a number of paranormal, ghostly and Gothic horror novels and novellas.

Her novels include: *The Stones of Landane, Those Who Dwell in Mordenhyrst Hall, The After-Death of Caroline Rand, Nemesis of the Gods* trilogy: *Wrath of the Ancients, Waking the Ancients,* and *Damned by the Ancients, Dark Observation, In Darkness, Shadows Breathe, The Garden of Bewitchment. The Haunting of Henderson Close, The Devil's Serenade, The Pendle Curse* and *Saving Grace Devine*.

The Crow Witch and Other Conjurings is a collection of her previously published and brand new short stories.

Her novellas include: *The Darkest Veil, Linden Manor, Cold Revenge, Miss Abigail's Room, The Demons of Cambian Street, Dark Avenging Angel, The Devil Inside Her,* and *The Second Wife.*

She lives by the sea in Southport, England with her long-suffering husband, and a black cat called Serafina who has never forgotten that her species used to be worshipped in ancient Egypt. She sees no reason why that practice should not continue.

You can connect with Cat here:

Website: catherinecavendish.com/
Facebook: facebook.com/CatherineCavendishWriter
X (formerly Twitter): twitter.com/Cat_Cavendish
Instagram: instagram.com/catcavendish/
Tik Tok: catcavendish
Bluesky @catcavendish.bsky.social

Curious about other Crossroad Press books? Stop by our website: http://crossroadpress.com

We offer quality writing

in digital, audio, and print formats.

Subscribe to our newsletter on the website homepage and receive a free eBook.